P9-EIE-437

THE GREAT AMERICAN WRITING BLOCK

Causes and Cures of the New Illiteracy

THOMAS C. WHEELER

THE VIKING PRESS
New York

CARNEGIE LIBRARY
LIVINGSTONE COLLEGE
SALISBURY, N. C. 28144

ACKNOWLEDGMENTS

Holt, Rinehart and Winston: From "The Gift Outright" from *The Poetry of Robert Frost* edited by Edward Connery Lathem. Copyright 1942 by Robert Frost. Copyright © 1969 by Holt, Rinehart and Winston. Copyright © 1970 by Lesley Frost Ballantine. From "Acquainted with the Night" from *The Poetry of Robert Frost* edited by Edward Connery Lathem. Copyright 1928, © 1969 by Holt, Rinehart and Winston. Copyright © 1956 by Robert Frost. Reprinted by permission of Holt, Rinehart and Winston, Publishers.

Mrs. Robert Linscott: From "The Soul Selects Her Own Society" and "I'm Nobody! Who Are You?" by Emily Dickinson.

The New York Times: From "Getting Out, and Up," by Peter J. Rondinone. Copyright © 1976 by the New York Times Company.

Random House, Inc., and Alfred A. Knopf, Inc.: From "Poems of Our Climate" from *The Collected Poems of Wallace Stevens*, Copyright 1942 by Wallace Stevens and renewed © 1970 by Holly Stevens. From "Many Happy Returns" from *Collected Poems* by W. H. Auden, edited by Edward Mendelson, Copyright 1945 by W. H. Auden.

Copyright © Thomas C. Wheeler, 1979

All rights reserved

First published in 1979 by The Viking Press
625 Madison Avenue, New York, N.Y. 10022
Published simultaneously in Canada by
Penguin Books Canada Limited

Library of Congress Cataloging in Publication Data
Wheeler, Thomas C
    The great American writing block.
    1. Language arts—United States.
2. Illiteracy—United States. I. Title.
LB1576.W486   420′.7′1073   79–14298
ISBN 0–670–34839–2

Printed in the United States of America
Set in Videocomp Times Roman

The
Great
American
Writing
Block

Edited by Thomas C. Wheeler

A VANISHING AMERICA:
THE LIFE AND TIMES OF THE SMALL TOWN

THE IMMIGRANT EXPERIENCE:
THE ANGUISH OF BECOMING AMERICAN

420.7
W 564

FOR MY WIFE, CAROL,
AND MY SON, NICHOLAS

$7.52
BT1
8-26-80

110074

Acknowledgments

Without classes to give and students to teach, this book could not have been written. I'm grateful to students at the City University of New York and especially grateful to those whose writing I have used here. To American writers who have nourished me, I maintain a debt that I hope is somehow honored in passages here. In the long journey from manuscript to book, Zev Shanken, Dick Pollak, Philip Winsor, Grace Shaw, Alden Cohen, and Barbara Rhodes have given me encouragement. I am especially grateful to my editors, Susan Zuckerman and Richard Seaver, for their commitment and effective comment.

Contents

Something we were withholding made us weak
Until we found out that it was ourselves
We were withholding from our land of living . . .
                    —Robert Frost in *The Gift Outright*

"Oh, but when you are tired it will be easier for you to talk English."
"American."
"Yes American. You will please talk American. It is a delightful language."
                    —Ernest Hemingway in *A Farewell to Arms*

A myth, like competition, brings out the best in a man.
        —A student in the SEEK program at York College

The
Great
American
Writing
Block

1 The Writing Crisis

Language in America. What today inhibits the writing of citizens, scholars, and students? Americans, long vigorous and inventive in speech, object to the act of writing. Two out of three abilities expected from education—reading and writing—disintegrate as some insidious influence, thought by many to be television, captures succeeding generations of children. Many grade schools and high schools no longer encourage self-expression or sentences. Finding entering freshmen unable to write clearly and coherently, colleges teach grammar and development of thought in a salvage operation called Remedial Writing. But even college graduates come into the job market unable to write, fearful of writing.

At the University of California at Berkeley, where students come from the top 12.5 percent of high school graduating classes, nearly half the entering freshmen display such inadequacies in writing that they are required to take remedial courses. At the University of Michigan and the University of Georgia, as at many colleges, remedial writing replaces the one term of freshman English common a decade ago. Even graduate students have writing problems. Purdue University tests all advanced-degree candidates with a writ-

1

ten essay exam in order to determine whether they can write acceptable English.

A nationwide study of writing ability in 1969–70 that examined the passages submitted by 94,000 schoolchildren and young adults found that not many "moved beyond basic constructions and commonplace language." Five years later, in 1975, a recheck found the essays of thirteen- and seventeen-year-olds more awkward, disorganized, and incoherent. These adjectives also describe the writing of many freshmen at the City University of New York, where I am a teacher.

The writing crisis has been getting worse. In defense of literacy, every wordsmith has his own horror story to tell. In a scrawled note, a bright girl, not long out of high school, wished me a "Mary Christmas." An editor of a national weekly told me she would be wary of hiring a copy editor under thirty, for fear of grammatical incompetence. A doctor, judging me physically fit and confiding a woe of his, deplored the inability of medical students he teaches to express themselves clearly in writing. An architect of my generation tells me that bright young architects he has hired cannot put a coherent report together. Although the young resent it, their elders utter more than the usual complaints of an older generation against the language of a new.

No one doubts that the high schools teach less than ever before. A colleague tells me that her son, who wrote imaginative short stories in a private elementary school, is not asked to write anything in one of New York City's special high schools for the academically superior. My students, from high schools lower on the scale, tell me more. They have never heard of a run-on sentence. Although some had been asked to write one-page essays every so often, the essays were apparently not corrected. The clumsiest, most incompetent writers have told me "English" was their best high school subject (a mystery I cannot unravel), while those who made the most conspicuous progress and began to write forcefully told me they had hardly ever written before. With the exception of private schools, with the exception of "good" high schools that put "gifted" students in writing classes—with the exception of the exceptions—high schools have, for all practical purposes, abandoned composition. Teaching students to write an essay and to handle ideas is now left to colleges, which find, inevitably, that they must begin with basics.

If students are assigned a "classic" in high school English, a survey by *The New York Times* found, few of them read much of it; but then, few long, serious books are assigned today. Though the problem of sustained reading is grave enough, the inability to write coherently is catastrophic. A people who cannot express their thoughts in writing are in greater trouble than a people who don't read "classics." Without clear thinking and coherent writing, no society can function properly. The widespread ability to write—the civilizing result of the industrial revolution—is an underpinning that the technological age tries to destroy but needs for its survival.

Certainly the reading crisis is one cause of the writing problem. Students who find reading a chore will inevitably find writing difficult. When students enjoy reading, they gain not only a familiarity with language but respect for writing. Books that engage a student's interest enlarge his vocabulary and his mental experience. We should be concerned not only with declining reading scores but with the texts that are used to teach reading today. In many schools the reading of interesting books is replaced by technical training in "reading skills." Many of the reading texts are so jargon-filled and so divorced from real life that they discourage both reading and writing. Although reading is essential, writing requires more than an appreciation of books. Decent writing emerges from the mind's storage of words heard and read; it comes too from one's view of life. When, in the nineteenth century, Hawthorne "coldly" showed the young William Dean Howells his sparsely filled bookcase, Howells knew that Hawthorne prided himself in being a student of men more than of books. Search the shelves of many contemporary writers and find a modest collection of books that have shaped the writer's outlook and language. It is not the amount of reading a student has done but his involvement in it that helps his writing. To write—to write well or to write adequately —is to draw from one's whole experience. To come into command of writing is, finally, to use one's own voice, to empower it with one's own identity.

"This generation has grown up without learning concentration—you don't develop that by switching channels. What can teachers do but pander to the rapid alteration of mood and attention." This view, from the chairman of an academic committee on literacy, puts the blame on television. The tube easily becomes the boob—and certainly is one of the culprits—keeping people from reading and writing. But television does something worse than shorten the attention span. As others have suggested, excessive viewing may finally destroy parts of the mind. The greater violence of TV is not the successive scenes of physical violence, harmful as they may be, but the primacy of the visual. In reading and listening the mind must decode, and drawing in a whole situation, reproduce within its own cavern the scene that language depicts. Language taxes the intellect. The more the mind works with words—words read, words heard, words spoken—the stronger it is, the more able to read and write. Television limits the mental work of the viewer. While it does use language, it is often of a simple order; and while it does make noise, it is often Muzak-type music that lulls the viewer along. Surely a point is reached in excessive television viewing where the child ceases to think at all. By not using his brain, the child may lose the function of part of it. The passivity of the TV viewer, noted since the inception of TV, produces a debilitation of the species. Unless the television picture is used like the set in a good play—as background for language and foreground for acting—it weakens the image making, the decoding capacity of the mind. Only a great picture is worth a thousand words and then only the way a great love affair is—condensing, representing a life of emotion. Even if, instead of watching TV, a child spent half of each day in art galleries, he still wouldn't be better off. As much of television uses it, the visual is a desert without sand.

But instead of resisting technology, schools have invited it into the classroom. Audiovisual equipment, on which millions of federal dollars have been spent, may be helpful to the handicapped, but it simplifies language in the way television does; and it implicitly discourages the use of books.

The writing and reading crises are too widespread among people of varying backgrounds to put the blame on television alone or primarily. The visual has come to dominate not only entertainment, but schoolbooks as well. Early reading texts once were dominated by words in bold letters, and used illustrations incidentally; now the visual often overwhelms the language. Comic books have orderly captions compared to some early reading texts whose sentences float in a sea of illustration. As does television, predominantly visual reading texts deprive the child of his own image making, and dissipate ideas into design. Action-oriented, even psychedelic in color—as if a child's attention could be arrested only by blinking neon—some texts become *Sesame Street* in print. If given relief from the visual assault, children could still find refuge and learning in the grip of unadulterated language. As some schools still do, all schools could build a world of books and language in which a child's mind could flourish. But the further grade school teaching goes, the more technological it becomes. To test a child's reading ability and to prepare him for test taking, purely informational texts replace the art of stories. Just as television breaks a half hour into bits, so reading texts offer only short, unrelated passages. Television presents the child with worlds with which he can have no real relationship, but the data-crammed paragraphs simply bore him. Other countries continue to educate with an emphasis on language and literature, but we have become too much of a "with it" nation to keep educational traditions.

As devastating an influence as television is the objective test system, introduced by higher learning—and now used in secondary education. Until the 1950s, students wrote essays in schools because they were expected to write essays on college entrance exams. But the university abandoned the essay requirement by adopting, a generation ago, the entirely objective test for admission, the Scholastic Aptitude Test (SAT).* Before World War II the objective SAT had been a supplement to written Achievement Tests in various subjects. But when the SAT became dominant, the Achievement Tests became objective too.† When the university dropped the essay requirement, it failed to recognize the power of the system it launched. Once the college entrance exams were objective, secondary schools asked for less writing. Urged on by test manufacturers, high schools began to use objective tests not only to prepare their students, but for their own examinations. The university, by sanctioning the objective system, bears a terrible responsibility for the decline of writing in the United States.

Today, the test manufacturers—led by the Educational Testing Service of Princeton, N. J.—are big businesses profiting from miseducation. ETS produces not only the SAT, but a battery of tests used for secondary and graduate education. Although the tests have made writing seem unnecessary— although they have also damaged reading ability—they are too expensive to throw out or replace. Harmful though the tests are, the schools have submitted to a system that runs on its own power. Measuring students means measuring schools—according to the aggregate scores of the enrolled— and few schools dare drop out of the spiral of relative standing. Public schools are also tied to the tests by school boards demanding measurement.

Developed first for the Army in World War I and widely used in World War II to test intelligence and ability, objective tests are gifts of war to civilian life. In the twenty-five years the SAT has been dominant, American education has

---

*Most American colleges use the SAT; some, mainly in the South and West, use the American College Test (ACT), developed later, modeled after the SAT, and produced by the American College Testing Program of Iowa City. Some colleges accept scores on either. Since the SAT is the prototype, it is this dominant test that is discussed in this book.
†The Achievement Tests also became optional. The change from the written essay to objective Achievement Tests in History and the Social Sciences was catastrophic. Such subjects, drawing greater student interest than English, had required and brought forth solid writing abilities.

been revolutionized. The marketplace has overturned the traditional foundations of learning—reading and writing— more completely than the efforts of any mechanistic theorist. Most Americans are probably tested more than they are taught. Composition, essay questions, term papers—vigorous thinking—all have yielded to one right answer out of four, to boxes to be checked, blanks to be filled. Objective tests not only carry the prestige of being scientifically accurate—when they aren't—but are also an easy way of handling the masses by machine. The results might have been predictable to an educational system that valued education. The national SAT Verbal Aptitude scores have shown a steady decline over a ten-year period. If the scores are worth anything, they show how poor a teacher objective tests are. The American language—supple, imaginative, and alive— has lost ground to the pretense of measurement. "Nobody ever cared about my writing," is a refrain I, as a teacher, have heard in several accents. After two decades of objective education, the "educationally disadvantaged" are not merely the poor and minority groups, but the supposedly well-educated and the well-to-do.

In the past, writing was not so much "taught" as shown. In the nineteenth century the Bible, widely read, influenced Americans to write declaratively, simply, imaginatively. Newspapers and radio played their roles in teaching as biblical Elizabethan, the origin of American language, lost its regular audience. Much nostalgic reverence is now given to *McGuffey's Readers* and to New England primers in the name of honoring basics, but the old texts didn't preach grammatical rules; they presented young readers with lively, clear texts on American situations. Symptomatic of today's approach, most grammar books list rules and principles, amplifying the order of a dictionary. Grammar itself becomes a specialty divorced from its use. In the past, reading more, students enjoyed more of what they read, and hearing more conversation than a TV tube produces, soaked in the syntax of language. Since they were asked to write throughout school, they learned from writing, as well as from reading and hearing. The horrendous misspellings of freshmen today—*probaly, satify;* the endless confusions of *there* for *their,* of *where* for *were,* of *went* for *gone*—result not from the demise of the spelling bee, but from rarely having written words down.

When reading is not habitual but a forced drill, and when grammar is a distant abstraction, years of vacancy have to be filled by one, two, or three semesters of—to use the ugly word—remediation. At the college level no one has ever had to "teach" writing before. Even twenty years ago, a fair time for the literary teacher, freshman English was a literature course in which students who had been writing for ten years perfected style and punctuation. Today, faced with the need to teach the unpracticed, colleges turn the mute over to English faculties trained for literary scholarship, who are appalled by the new ignorance, and often temperamentally hostile to it. Teachers, however, can insist that students have meaningful experiences to write about; and experience can be explored in the first writing assignments. In spite of early resistance within the academic community, remedial teaching actually has gotten better and has begun to work. Adapting to a different job, more and more English faculty have come to recognize that education begins with and builds on what a student already knows, however invisible that knowledge may seem to be.

But, wherever they begin to write steadily and seriously, Americans encounter a subtle psychological barrier in the name still used for the practice of reading and writing—English. Our language is indisputably American—distinctive not in its grammar, when correct, but in its idiom and brisk pace. The student, young or old, faces a forbidding title for the tongue he is to write. The bold and well-educated can cope with it; but others, schooled badly or well, can be easily intimidated. It is not ethnicity that makes "English" a tough name to meet, it is the native Americanness of all of us. "English" encourages in many young Americans, unconsciously but doggedly, the evasion of a foreign tongue. For teachers upholding standards of "English," the title invites teaching by rules, regulations, and finally formulas. Colonial rule has to be imposed. Throughout American history there has been a smoldering rebellion against the "English" of the classroom. With only partial success, schoolmarms chided the country boys; and in cities, civil servants tried to cleanse the immigrants. Huck Finn was—and remains—a prototype of resistance to "correct" English, of loyalty to a spoken language. Against the language of technology, against "English" too, students now revolt in an anarchy of usage, a sloppiness of expression.

The illiteracy crisis is even more tragic in light of the old glory of the American language. (Because of American isolation, the influence of the Bible on our language lasted longer than on British English; in England new styles succeeded one another. Even in our earthiness we are still heirs of the Elizabethans.) Faced from the beginning with new conditions of life, the American has had to adapt English words to American necessities and to coin words of his own. Our idiom expresses our history, our humanity. First the English and then the American academics inveighed against American innovations, and then finally adopted them. Thomas Jefferson was flailed in a London review in 1787 for writing *to belittle,* but the verb, like so many brisk Americanisms, became so common in England that in 1862 it appeared in Trollope. As H. L. Mencken noted in *The American Language* (1937), ". . . the American, on his linguistic side, likes to make his language as he goes along, and not all the hard work of the schoolmarm can hold the business back. A novelty loses nothing by the fact that it is a novelty; it rather gains something, and particularly if it meets the national fancy for the terse, the vivid, and, above all, the bold and the imaginative." Commending "the superior imaginativeness revealed by Americans in meeting linguistic emergencies," Mencken charted the course of American creativity in response to a new environment, meeting the needs of a necessarily direct people. From the town meeting to the political caucus, from the backwoods to the frontier, from the railroad, the barroom, the jazz band, and now the ghetto (all previous terms are themselves mild examples of American inventions or conversions), the uneducated as well as the educated have created an American language fitting our circumstances and energy. The string of native idioms and compounds that trip off our American tongues, that no English or academic soap has been able to wash away, is infinite and ongoing. Consider *back talk* and *downtown, to peter out,* and *to fly off the handle* as nineteenth-century creations; *scofflaw* and *sit-in, splashdown* and *drop out* as twentieth-century word building. *Spellbinders* and *screwballs, shortstops* and *shortcuts,* and countless thousands of Americanisms have *taken hold* and are *here to stay.* Although the line must surely be held against American barbarisms, of which illiteracy is one and useless slang another, some who teach "English" really teach American without appreciating the native genius.

As new usages came into speech, nineteenth-century American writers—leaving bad grammar to dialogue—took up the most useful and expressive of them. Literature, as it had in other nations, became the authority. If American literature were more consistently read in our schools, it might exercise some authority over student writing. But English is not only the nametag for composition courses; English literature is still the specialty of most teachers in colleges and in high schools. Though American literature has come more into favor in the classroom, it is still a body of work most students never meet.

The struggle to claim American language has gone on for a long time. Nineteenth-century American writers—Cooper, Howells, Twain, and Whitman—publicly pled the cause against native Anglophiles. In 1924 Rupert Hughes, the critic, was sufficiently outraged by the Anglophiles to write, in *Harper's Magazine,* "Let us put off the livery, cease to be the butlers of another people's language, and try to be the masters and creators of our own"—even while Hemingway, Fitzgerald, Dos Passos were doing just that. In 1923, Robert Frost, then perfecting an American idiom, denied that

American poetry came from either "the soil" or "the city," from "the native" or "the alien." He said in an interview, "Where there is life there is poetry, and just as much as our life is different from English life, so is our poetry different. . . . When he [the immigrant] becomes articulate and raises his voice in the outburst of song, he is singing an American lyric. He is an American. His poetry is American. He could not have sung that same song in the place from where he hails; he could not have sung it in any other country to which he might have emigrated. Be grateful for the individual note he contributes and adopt it for your own as he has adopted the country."

Mencken noted in 1937, "The popular speech is pulling the exacter speech along and no one familiar with its suc- cesses in the past can have much doubt that it will succeed again, soon or late." Decent American writing has always resulted from a tension between the vulgar—what Mencken called "the great reservoir of the language"—and educated speech. But educated writing—often a product of graduate schools—veers from the popular language. Let the two sepa- rate entirely and the written language will fade further, the popular speech further decline. The two must be in some equilibrium for either to be safe.

Teaching American might bring better results than teach- ing English; and the least our professors should do is to call the language American English, as some already do, or call it the American language. Teaching writing—because writ- ing is inevitably self-expression—is always touchy, because the student's ego is at stake and is easily offended. How terrible, then, to ignore his national history by giving him an English bath.

In his 1837 American Scholar Address, Emerson urged Americans to turn away from "the courtly muses of Europe." That same year he noted in his *Journal:*

The language of the street is always strong. What can describe the folly and emptiness of scolding like the word *jawing?* I feel too the force of the double negative, though clean contrary to our grammar rules. And I confess to some pleasure from the stinging rhetoric or a rattling oath in the mouths of truckmen and teamsters. How laconic and brisk it is by the side of a page of The North Atlantic Review. Cut these words and they would bleed; they are vascular and alive; they walk and they run. Moreover they who speak have this elegancy, that they do not trip in their speech. It is a shower of bullets; whilst the Cambridge men and Yale men correct themselves and begin again at every half sentence.

The passage is a good example of the tendencies of written American. The sentences are declarative, falling without formula more to brevity than to length. American comes up short to clinch a point. One thinks of Thoreau surfacing from rivers of prose: "The mass of men lead lives of quiet desperation." Even in the delicious lengths of Thoreau and W. E. B. Du Bois—the latter not yet valued as an American writer—American has a love for thrift of phrase. As in the Emerson passage, briskness comes from the verbs. *Cut, bleed, walk, run, trip*—active and plain—are metaphors lifted from a physical life. A nation, much of whose history is physical endeavor, has the physical in its language. The vernacular—*stinging, rattling, shower of bullets*—stands side by side with more formal terms; energy comes from the pairing. There is nothing dull or common about the passage because it reaches into letters and life. The language of the street will never write an essay, but the ear of the good writer is tuned by it. Students of writing, however, are usually drowned in vocabulary lists. They are not thought to have an ear or a language of their own. They think they must use big words, and their writing becomes, predictably, tedious and impersonal. They are taught only half the mixture.

Contemporary novelists, such as Ellison and Bellow, conscious heirs of Emerson's nationalism, honor the popular language as well as their educated vocabularies. The best American journalism today is also written in a mixture of the formal and colloquial. But in the classroom, as in textbooks, American language is edged out by academic jargon—the bulky phraseology of psychologists, the heavy abstractions of social science. At a faculty meeting, an English medievalist laces his talk with street language; but English professors, perhaps even the medievalist, preach the doctrine: *Never write as you speak.* In telling students to forget their natural speech, teachers ask them to forget everything, for their voices contain far more than slang. Under that academic prohibition, speech can never rise through the mind. In the speaking voice lies the miracle, the beginning of writing. Even the illiterate, when they talk of something they care about, perform feats of grammar and thought—by the sentence, by the paragraph.

Once, at an English Department meeting, I suggested that teaching primarily by rules and regulations blocked the powers of the mind. "How are you going to tell a student," one Ph.D. asked, "that the following sentence is wrong: 'The reason for the student being late was because the subway broke down'?" Another Ph.D. replied, "Two noun clauses cannot go together." But these grammarians had lost sight of the power of the human voice. When students write, as they often do at the beginning, "the reason . . . was because," they only display that gap bred in their minds between written and spoken language. When I tell students to *write as directly as you speak* such contortions of language clear up. They invariably write, "The student was late because the subway broke down." To many academics, the speaking voice is a barbarous instrument, to be silenced in writing. But writing is not simply a transcription of the speaking voice; it is a heightening of it in that time that writing allows for thought.

Linguists—the "new linguists"—now believe that grammar is not an act of imitation but an innate ability, inborn, emerging in a child's first speech. When they first begin to speak, children use verbs and speak in sentences. Writers have guessed for a long time what linguists now postulate: Grammar is a set of names for the way the mind works with language. For descriptive purposes the names come in handy. But teaching by rules alone does not give the student confidence in his own voice. The first emphasis must be on encouraging the student to use the voice. It contains the miracle of grammar. Particulars that the voice has not mastered must be learned through workbook exercises and through instruction. The more of this a student can do for himself, prodded by the instructor, the more he will learn.

One year when New York State budget cuts threatened York College—one of the four-year colleges in the City University of New York and the college where I teach—I acted upon an administrative suggestion and asked students to write letters to the legislature supporting full funding of the school. All the letters began, "It has come to my attention that . . ." When I pointed out the methodical beginnings, students who were now writing essays with competence and sometimes individuality replied, "That's the way we were taught in Business English."

Some subspecies of "Business English" is becoming more and more common. At the Watergate hearings, Nixon's bright young men with their *points in time* would *depart Camp David* and *arrive Key Biscayne* without knowing the difference between an intransitive verb, requiring a preposition, and a transitive one, capable of a direct object. Their verbs came from the airport terminal. Science, which has discovered its truths detail by detail, step by step, has become in the minds of nonscientists something to imitate—not its method but its labeling and classification system. The weak, alas, misunderstand the strong. Psychologists seeking categories, imitating science, write a jargon concealing all clarity; in some of their inventions—*cognitive imagery, perceptual dysfunction, personality feedback*—people are described like machines. Academic jargon is infected with computer terminology—*program feedback, committee input*—even while English professors are still caught in Latinate imitations. From professional schools of education comes "educationese," such as this professional analysis of a classroom situation: "Her result was a confusion matrix showing how often these children confuse each letter with every other letter." The greater the oppression of language, the more assertive the folk language—and the more form is abused.

American English has fallen not just to sentence fragments but to incomplete talk. The young talk less well because they write less, because vigorous speech has been tested or stolen away.

Still, in spite of the colonial rule of English and the tyranny of tests, Americans haven't given up on literary expression. Today, Americans hanker after the act of individuality that writing should be. "To write" is even the dream of many who will, alas, continue to mangle the language. A young lady whom I had coached through a remedial course told me a couple of years later that she hoped to publish some of her "literary works." Colleges find that less pretentious students, once they have completed basic work, often want more courses in writing. English Departments, once snobbish even about creative writing and journalism courses but finding fewer students interested in English literature electives, now find that they can stay in business by offering courses in nonfiction writing. Some faculties, further losing the struggle for humanity in language, and catering to new fashion, call their courses "Communications." Here, it seems, students may learn at last, like radio towers, to send out impressive sounds. The flood of writers' conferences, writers' schools, and writing courses in and out of college attests to the frantic effort of many Americans to be somebody through language. Writing the novel, the play, or the poem has been the underground hope of businessmen as well as the vocation of Bohemians. In a country that reads little poetry, an enormous amount of poetry is written. American language has built American song, a street poetry, for generations. The best popular music has always had style and content. A decent respect for writing in our schools would strengthen many willing hands. Those who write well only exercise their individuality. Self-expression, in spite of our difficulty with the written word, still proves as fundamentally American as cutting down cherry trees.

When, in 1952, I left college with only a Master's degree, an English professor swore that should I ever want to teach I'd be teaching nothing more than Freshman Composition. With some luck as a lubricant, I have wriggled out of that dreary prediction into the higher realms of advanced writing, of literature itself, but lately I have concentrated on the remedial job. When, after earning my living as a journalist, after free-lancing and not earning enough, I did turn to teaching, revelations occurred in the dramas of Freshman Composition. The longer I taught the more I was drawn toward teaching minorities to hear strong sounds of speech. At Brooklyn College, where I began teaching, a number of Orthodox Jews clad in sports coats and yarmulkes occupied one of my evening classes. Attending Yeshivas (religious schools) by day, they had been brought up on the Book, and in the endless talmudic dialogues had learned to ask questions. Wearing fedoras on top of yarmulkes in the secular hallways, they were self-confident exiles holding to a belief —one told me—that had saved their parents from the Nazi persecution. But it was not the power of God in them that drew me; it was their implicit identity. Identity—a cube of ice, unmeltable, at the center of oneself, formed from all sorts of sources—is a force that allows every writer—even students of writing—to write well. But some of the Orthodox Jews, like other students who had been "successful" in high school, were so hung up in formulas, had become such induction and deduction machines, that they had to remove their intellectual showcases before writing well.

Among other students, there were individuals who stood out, who brought identity to their writing. Out of the Vietnam war came a T-shirted, red-haired young man writing tales about his role in a tangled war. A slim, long-haired girl who considered herself inarticulate came to life—danced like the dancer she was—in a paper on Thoreau.

Then, as the admission policy broadened in the early 1970s, bringing students with low high school averages into the city colleges, I began teaching a course in a program called SEEK (Search for Education, Elevation, and Knowledge), designed for ill-prepared black and Puerto Rican students. I didn't have a romance with the nonstandard grammar called black dialect, but I was drawn by the identity in these aroused, committed students. Many of my students had failed in the educational system of tests—or had never learned to take them. But they were able to speak forcefully and could summon an eloquence, a lyricism, when encouraged to write. In many of the poor, spirit was accessible; it hadn't been taught away. And spirit, of course, is the song of identity. Both, I knew, had something to do with suffering, and with that I had some sympathy. The ability to admit to suffering quickens all the sensibilities. If we cannot admit to hurt—perhaps man's deepest experience—the whole self freezes. Joy is the first and self-expression the ultimate loss. I've found the spirit congealed and writing blocked in enough middle-class sons and daughters—black as well as white—to suspect a deeper problem than tests, television, or "English." The writing crisis is finally a crisis of identity in which tests and television, schools and a blur of culture conspire. The spell of advertisements, the plastic slipcovers, all those illusions of happiness in America so cheaply for sale —a culture of optimism ignoring complexity—all have wrought a denial of self. All those securities we use to hide from some dreadful truth muffle our ability to ask questions of the world, to react, to write.

Whenever I have found a profound writing problem in a student—writing little, never developing a thought, losing a thread in incoherence—it has been a problem of psyche or soul. A curtain has dropped between what the student admits and what his mind might tell him. A girl with much definition in her face, grace in her movement, the ability to concentrate, but unaccountably clumsy in her writing, pierced the chaos when she said of an unclear point, "I'm hiding from that." To teach writing is to provoke or cajole, to nurse or embarrass the American from his hiding place. It is to show him that he does have an identity—a way of looking at the world that is uniquely his and that in writing becomes a point of view, an organizing force. To get him to reveal himself is to get him to talk, in the classroom if possible—if necessary, to himself as he writes. To get him to talk is to show him that he has a language of his own that he can put to work in writing.

Occasionally breaking into a doubting smile, one black student never missed a class, but rarely wrote the assignments. Heavyset, wearing the white uniform of a student nurse, she wrote in a slow and tortured way; the words came out like drops from the last wringing of laundry. Asked to render an impression of something she had seen and thought about during the recent spring vacation, she sat immobile until the closing moments of the class and finally wrote:

> Walking down 125th Street looking in all the African store windows, I started to dream.
>
> I saw my family in beautifully styled African clothes. We were living in Africa happy and free. There were many tall beautiful trees and flowers of all sizes, all colors it was a breathtaking sight. There were children lots of children all happy laughing running and playing.
>
> The women were shopping and working in their gardens with their vegetables and flowers. The men were working, some in politics others worked the mines some were computer operators. Many of the men worked in factories a few made their living in the sea. I have this dream many times it cheers me up.

In her vision of a black Eden she had reached into feeling and at last found the courage to write. Because she had found in her fantasy a subject that mattered to her, she had found balance in her writing. She had begun to use commas and periods, though not consistently.

As usual, the assignments were designed to help the student express his identity; in the SEEK classes self-expression rose easily, and if it found a meaningful subject, it glided toward literacy and sometimes way beyond. Elusive thing, identity had better be more than a gut reaction; at best it is expressed as an attitude, a way of looking at the world.

The next term a Puerto Rican girl brought irony and grievance to bear in a passage written in class. Short and olive-skinned, her hair a gleaming black, looking a bit like a girl not too far from her first communion, she seemed to move, to glide, in a world of feeling. Perhaps she would never write a scholarly paper on Jonathan Swift, but she too was a satirist of poverty.

In order for anyone to know why I behave the way I do he must know something about the beautiful place where I was born. I was born in the most beautiful place in the world where the sidewalks are lined with garbage cans and the people are all trouble free. Everyone wears a smile to hide the pain, the tears, and the disillusion. There is music and laughter everywhere so you won't hear the cries of anguish. I was born in "Harlem." It is very important for you to know this. I do not have the same morals as a middle class person would. We were born in different worlds. Worlds so close and yet so far. I have been made to understand the middle class values and yet my values have been ignored. They say we are sick, underprivileged. I say we are not the ones who are sick, you are. We have just adapted to life.

In middle-class students I had seen some morals I deplored, though perhaps not those she had in mind. Cheating occurred. I kept on getting term papers on "Capital Punishment" identical to ones that had been turned in before. Once I received a term paper on *Walden* so familiar that I could look it up; passage by passage, it was taken from a Brooks Atkinson introduction to Thoreau. I rose to a Puritan punishment. The girl had been an *A* student, but now all her work lay in the shadow of doubt. Just after turning in an *F* grade for her for the term, I met her in the hallway. "My mother gave it to me to turn in," she said of the paper. "My sister had used it once, and my mother said if it was good enough for her, why don't you turn it in, if you don't have anything else." She swore, as the tears threatened to come down, that all the other papers were hers alone. "I've got to get a good mark. My parents will kill me if I don't." After a brisk lecture which brought a vow of obedience from her, I remitted her *F* and gave her the gift of a *B*. A week later I got a thank-you card, white with embossed white lettering, just signed with her name.

The pressures to succeed by any means are employed at great cost. This student had worked hard in high school for the 85 average then necessary for admission to the City University. If education didn't involve her, was she involved in cheating? Behind her were her parents—hard-working no doubt—afraid they'd lose the little they hoped for, afraid that something would happen to deprive their daughter of an American door prize.

When a Puerto Rican girl in a SEEK class turned in a term paper that same term on, of all topics, the "Puritan Tradition," my suspicions were so aroused that I accused her of stealing it right out of the library. I was wrong. My suspicion was in part founded on her waifish look—a thin brown figure with her shirttail always hanging out—as well as on her new literacy. Ah, prejudice; having felt cheated by whites, I picked on her. She held back the tears the guilty offer under such accusations. "I worked on it hard. I worked on it very hard." In my SEEK class I had been struck by the students' integrity and had begun to romanticize ethnic pride. It couldn't allow for the desperation of upward mobility apparent in some of the white students. Prejudice in reverse.

The next term a pretty black girl turned in a paper I had received word for word several times from whites. Dressed in flowery chintz, sitting there like a bored azalea queen, she was a Southern belle raiding the Northern encyclopedias.

Then there was Mrs. Smith, a very black and bony lady of unbridled determination. For her paper on *The Scarlet Letter* she turned in whole paragraphs from Hawthorne's introduction. "But Mrs. Smith, these are Hawthorne's sentences," I protested earnestly. She gathered herself together in mumbles and whispered, "I can write as well as anyone else." Mrs. Smith was having a bad time with her writing. She had taken an earlier composition course with me two terms in a row, since I hadn't been able to pass her the first time. Now she honored me again by coming into the final remedial course. Because she had children at home and needed a baby-sitter, she paid to come to what was then a tuition-free college. She would rewrite a paper three times to prove her competence; and if she couldn't prove it any other way, she would finally copy out of a book and feel that she owed no one any apologies. At least it was a book we were both reading. There was nothing underhanded about her. "I'm coming here to get an education, and all the teachers tell me I'm not ready. Well, I'm as good as the next person, and you can't tell me I'm not." That spoken sentence was OK, and maybe, just maybe, she learned something not only from our encounter, but from copying an American master who used periods. Ben Franklin, ignorant youth and aspiring printer, perfected his writing by copying Addison and Steele. I don't suggest she'll go far copying Hawthorne or anyone else. Colonists before the Revolution and Americans for some years afterward could look only to Britain for models of style and polish. At least Mrs. Smith hadn't copied an exotic English modernist—an assignment on D. H. Lawrence might have stopped her entirely.

2 The Failure of Objectivity

Only the requirement to write, week by week, year by year, throughout grammar and high school, will produce literate Americans. But objective tests replace the act of writing; practice books and workbooks corrupt the language, and reading tests and texts often set insipid examples of writing.

"Because so many high school graduates are handicapped in college by the inability to express themselves," announced a leading training booklet for the nationwide SAT, "the College Entrance Board introduced a new type of test several years ago." It was called a "Writing Sample," and though it was a voluntary written exam, it was never graded, didn't affect admission, and was only occasionally used by a college—*after* acceptance—to determine whether a student needed remedial work. It was finally dropped because of disuse. The College Board had merely acknowledged the toll of twenty-five years of objective testing—and then proceeded to look for new ways of proving the illiteracy.

The Educational Testing Service of Princeton, New Jersey, which produces all the College Board examinations, came up with a new device in 1974 called "The Test of Standard Written English" (TSWE). This multiple choice test also ranks students according to an "objective" standard of competence. Oddly, it reinforces the curious notion that in order to write, a student need not actually write. "This score," ETS announced, "is not intended to be used by colleges in making admissions decisions but is meant to help place you in an appropriate freshman English course." Such an approach encourages secondary schools to continue to neglect writing; the responsibility for teaching writing is being passed to colleges. It is in college remedial writing programs that the serious teaching of writing can begin.

Neither ETS nor its parent body, the College Board, acknowledges that its tests encourage illiteracy. In a feeble attempt to appease criticism that there was no actual writing on these tests, ETS introduced in 1977 a twenty-minute essay at the end of the multiple-choice English Composition Achievement Test; the essay is included in only one of the five English tests given each year. Only 85,000 students (of the 206,000 who took achievement tests of any kind) took the English test and wrote the 250-word essay. Compare these figures to the 1.1 million students who took the SAT in 1977. This minimal response on the part of ETS can in no way be construed as a return to writing requirements.

Many colleges now profess doubts about SAT scores, and say that in admissions considerations high school grades and teacher recommendation are more important. One distinguished liberal arts college, Bowdoin College in Maine, found there was no correlation between high test scores and college performance. Finding the "predictive value of standardized tests" questionable and test scores misleading, it has abandoned the test requirement for admission. Of students graduating with honors in 1968 and 1969, Bowdoin found that less than a third scored above their class median while almost as many scored below; a few students with very low scores had graduated with distinction.* The Bowdoin study—and the skepticism of other colleges—challenge ETS's theory that the SAT "predicts" college performance. But prediction, true or false, is really a minor issue. The real point is that tests in "verbal ability" and "grammar" have also become the norm in high school testing.

In 1978, for the first time, responding perhaps to criticism of the test, the College Board released a sample SAT exam to students registering for the College Boards.† The test, it is often said, favors middle-class white students at the expense of minority groups. Certainly this is true. But middle-class blacks might do as well as their contemporaries on its verbal and mathematics sections. The SAT is not class-oriented as much as it is oriented toward already educated minds. Its tougher verbal questions can be conquered by informed guesswork, but often the correct answer depends on the sheer luck of the student's reading or experience. In a verbal section, the student is asked to "choose the word or phrase that is most nearly the *oppo-*

*Though applicants can still submit their test scores, Bowdoin dropped the requirement in order to deemphasize the tests, to put them in perspective, and to stress intangible "human qualities, many of them unmeasurable by aptitude and achievement tests." It stressed its interest in "the highly motivated student"; and it found the tests to be biased against minorities. In a poll asking Bowdoin faculty to name students with "qualities Bowdoin should be most eager to attract" and those students who were "models of what Bowdoin could do without," more than half of the undesirable students named had SAT scores higher than the class median. More often than not, apparently, Bowdoin faculty found a lack of character in high scorers. The new policy, established in 1970 and continuing today, was in part an effort to disabuse the public of the importance *it* attaches to SAT scores. For, in its policy statement, Bowdoin confessed to the failure of colleges "to communicate to candidates, schools, and parents the relatively subordinate role of College Board results in admission considerations." Clearly, at the instigation of a college system that requires the SAT, the American public seizes on scores as a form of triumph, or identity, in a mass society. Another institution of higher learning, the University of Wisconsin, has dropped the requirement of test scores for applicants. It has ceased requiring the SAT as well as the ACT. Its renunciation, however, did not question the predictability of the test scores. Wisconsin merely found that the scores did not add sufficient information to high school records to justify the small payment students must make to take them. The tests do not come off very well by that judgment either.

†The College Entrance Examination Board, the parent body of ETS, has a membership of 2300 colleges and secondary schools.

site in meaning to the word in capital letters." One example is this:

> WHET:
> A. expire
> B. heat
> C. delay
> D. slake
> E. revive

A student who didn't know the meaning of *slake,* the right answer, could still do well in college. Even if he didn't know the meaning but knew the precise meaning of *whet* and had prepared for the multiple-choice exam, he could get the right answer by process of elimination. On the accompanying answer sheet, ETS informs us that of students getting a slightly above median verbal score of 450* on this test, only 21 percent settled for *slake.*

In an analogies section, in which the student is asked to "select the lettered pair that best expresses a relationship similar to that expressed in the original pair," come these pairs:

> SWILL: SWINE
> A. roe: fish
> B. coop: poultry
> C. mutton: sheep
> D. pesticide: vermin
> E. fodder: cattle

If a student had read rural English novels or grown up on a farm, he would surely know what *swill* meant and make an instant connection with *fodder.* Only 28 percent of the near median scorers got *E,* the right answer. Since 450 is not a high SAT score, perhaps some poor farm boys succeeded where urban or suburban students failed.

*The median verbal score for the 1977–78 testing year was 429, a decline from the median score ten years ago of 462. In the same period the higher mathematics median score has declined somewhat less, from 494 to 468. A perfect score would be 800.

To give the devil his due, it must be said that the SAT asks for an ability to make fine distinctions, as in this analogy:

IMPREGNABLE: AGGRESSION
A. imperfect: revision
B. invisible: defense
C. inequitable: criticism
D. indivisible: separation
E. immutable: preservation

Thirty percent of the near median scorers chose the right answer, *D.* Just as something is *impregnable* against *aggression,* so is something *indivisible* if *separation* is tried.

SAT sentences, with their blanks filled in correctly, read well enough in this one released test; even the reading passages do not assault the ear of the sensitive reader. But even though verbal sections of the SAT are well enough written, the test is still obnoxious. Its verbal part, like other objective tests in language, does not ask for writing; and because it doesn't, the act of writing has withered in our schools.

Reading questions on the sample SAT try, with considerable success, to trick the student. Here is a paragraph from a longer passage on the sample test:

The way of the desert and the way of the jungle represent opposite methods of reaching stability at two extremes of density. In the jungle there is plenty of everything life needs except more space. Everything is on top of everything else; there is no cranny that is not both occupied and disputed. At every moment, war to the death rages fiercely. The place left vacant by any creature that dies is seized almost instantly by another, and life seems to suffer from nothing except too favorable an environment. In the desert, on the other hand, it is the environment itself which serves as the limiting factor. To some extent the struggle of creature against creature is mitigated, although it is of course not abolished even in the vegetable kingdom. For the plant which in one place would be strangled to death by its neighbor dies a thirsty seedling because that same neighbor has drawn the scant moisture from its spot of earth.

The question pertaining to this paragraph is:

Which of the following is (are) true of both the way of the jungle and the way of the desert?

> I. They are characterized primarily by the struggle of creature against creature.
> II. They are reactions to hostile environments.
> III. They result in population control.

(A) II only (B) III only (C) I and II only (D) II and III only (E) I, II, and III

What is a student, in a limited time, to do with these choices? The instructions tell the student to answer "on the basis of what is *stated* or *implied,*" but there is both a statement and an implication to reckon with. The testmakers undoubtedly intended to lure many students to *I, They are characterized primarily by the struggle of creature against creature.* For not only is the struggle a clear characteristic of both desert and jungle; it is also emphasized in the last sentence. But strong as that temptation may be, the student who yields to it will be wrong. For the testmakers have cleverly inserted the word *primarily* and linked *I* with the unacceptable possibility of *II.* To score well, the student must have his guard ready and high. The right answer is *B, They result in population control.* Perhaps the right answer is got by process of elimination. Or perhaps it is obtained by finding the faint implication in the phrases "reaching stability" and "limiting factor." To get the right answer in a short time does indicate something akin to the skill of a detective. But it does not indicate that a student could write a searching term paper. Getting the right answer does not measure the depth of a student's mind. Of those who scored 450, 20 percent succeeded. The skill of the testmakers would be far more acceptable if the exams also asked the student to write.

A clear use of language is inescapably a subjective act. The writer, from grade three to graduate school, must find in his own mind the words and the structure that express his meaning. The outside world—especially the delicious and lost art of reading—should make his mind worldly. Language and ideas must first sink in and be absorbed before the writer can deliver back the world's goods. Objective testing actively discourages the development of language within a student.

The objective test in writing, the released TSWE—the thirty-minute part of the SAT that is not counted in the SAT score—asks the student to spot the grammatical errors in underlined sections of sentences; it also asks him to choose from five possibilities the best way of phrasing an underlined part. In effect, the students are asked to be the cops when they are still the felons in any writing they actually perform. A student who can spot an error in an underlined section may still commit the same error in the frenzy of unaccustomed composition. Verbs will agree with subjects, pronouns with antecedents, only if students are involved in writing. Even if a student has a sure knowledge of grammar as shown on an objective test, the test still won't determine whether he can write an essay. For writing requires, as well as grammar, ideas and the ability to organize material. These abilities show up only in actual writing. The test is in many ways an exercise in futility. Good colleges will not use the score for placement purposes, as ETS recommends. Most colleges administer their own written essay exams to determine what level of composition course a student needs.

The Achievement Test in English Composition, taken in addition to the SAT if a student wishes to demonstrate "achievement" in English, is a multiple-choice exam concerned with terminology. Diligently, a student can mark errors in "diction," "usage," "idiom," "wordiness," "sentence structure," and "metaphor" without ever demonstrating that he can muster clarity, logic, or grace in his writing.

The test makes writing a spectator sport. Many good writers, students or not, are not whizzes at academic terminology but write well out of their sense of language. That kind of talent would do poorly on the test. The test itself encourages schools to teach primarily by terminology, since the final test asks for it. The student is asked to choose from several possibilities the right rephrasing of a sentence if a subordinate clause is changed to a participle, or if one sentence is changed to a clause. He is told, in effect, that writing is a juggling act, without purpose. Emphasis in a sentence occurs because of the meaning the writer has in mind. Reconstructing sentences, as the tests require, is truly a meaningless exercise. Led through a maze of single sentences, each with a maze of different possibilities for construction, the student might lose interest in language on the way.

ETS claims that the SAT measures "aptitude," but there are too many variables for that to occur. Much of what the test measures is acquired knowledge; "aptitude" in this case is learned. Since the test given varies from test date to test date, and since a student's experience vis-à-vis the questions asked will help determine his score, his score will depend on the particular test he takes. One ETS official claimed (but later denied) that there was a one-in-six chance that a student who scored 600 on one SAT one day could score 500 or 700 on another SAT the next day. Scores can be increased if a student studies for the exams. Cram schools and crash courses promise and produce higher scores. One New York City cram school has tables to prove that its thirty-hour course in vocabulary and reading-comprehension skills boost scores 50 to 100 points.* Just as the SAT has diminished writing in schools, so it has a spin-off in the marketplace. Leading educational publishers put out SAT practice books. Though the practice books can be helpful, the language of their tests sometimes becomes inaccurate and offensive.

*For much of my information here I am indebted to two articles on ETS, one by Steven Brill in *New York* magazine, October 7, 1974, and one by Ed Klemsh in *The Village Voice*, January 15, 1979.

The practice tests, the work of private educators who have studied ETS test descriptions, are used widely in high school crash courses as well as by individual students.* Their offenses of language are like those in high school workbooks and vocabulary builders. To witness an example of poor usage, take this "verbal pairs" from a practice test:

> The —— flower was also ——.
> A. pretty—redolent
> B. drooping—potable
> C. pale—opulent
> D. blooming—amenable

"The pretty flower was also redolent"—the "correct" answer—is by any count a stinking sentence. A sensible mind would easily light on *C:* "The pale flower was also opulent." Factually, this "wrong" choice is just as correct, for a peony or a rose can be both pale and opulent. The "wrong" sentence is actually right, since it goes beyond the obvious fact —it gets at irony, the deepest of truths. Even if a student chose the "wrong" sentence because it "sounded better," he would have exercised a basic judgment of writing. It does sound better, and is a better sentence. Sounds bind a sentence together into a logic of its own, pleasing the ear, easing the spirit. The *l* runs through the "wrong" sentence like water; *pale* and *also* prepare the way for the ironic idea of *opulent.* Redolent, in the "correct" sentence, comes up like an accident, with a crash.

The practice tests misuse language—and even allow grammatical errors to stand. In one practice test for the TSWE, the student is asked to circle the one error among all the underlined sections of this sentence: *"Anyone* with the *necessary* equipment can manufacture *their* own outdoor furniture; however, a certain degree of patience and skill *are also required."* The "right" solution is to pick *their,* since the pronoun should be *his* to agree with its singular antecedent,

*One publisher estimates that the practice books have an annual market of 250,000 —or about one fourth of the students who take the SAT.

anyone. But another problem of disagreement exists: *are also required* has a singular subject, *a certain degree.* A student who chose that error would be "wrong." Clumsy usage is shown in the blunderbuss of the word *manufacture.* The man in this sentence, using patience and skill, working certainly in a garage, basement, or backyard, could only "build" or "make" his own furniture, not "manufacture" it. To "manufacture" would require a factory producing a quantity. By using such language, the tests license bloated prose.

An Antonyms section often introduces words that are not the opposite to "the capitalized word" and issue an open invitation to foolish use. One practice test proclaims that the antonym of DECIDUOUS is "enduring"; its exact antonym, "coniferous," is not offered. Such elastic uses of language may encourage people to write, "President Nixon had a deciduous second term." *Agreement* is the "correct" antonym of POLEMIC according to the test. If so, taking license in the future, we may be able to say, "I had a strong polemic with you." The antonym of INVETERATE is, behold, *beginning.* All college catalogues should list Inveterate Writing Courses following the beginning ones.

The practice test questions are often couched in a formal language that offends the ear and obscures meaning. Sound and simplicity, directness and clarity—the great needs of writing—are sacrificed to the test mania. Speak, if you can, these Sentence Completions—with the "correct" word pairs here filled in from the choices offered. The sentences are insincere and cacophonic. "Because the scout took a *circuitous* route to get back to his platoon, the men felt considerable *apprehension* about his fate." One might believe the men felt "concern" if he had taken a "roundabout" route. "All his attempts to *eradicate* the offending spots proved *unavailing,* and he finally gave up in disgust." Perhaps if he had attempted merely to "remove" the spots, his efforts would not have been "futile." "The *mellifluous* tones of the flute succeeded in *soothing* his tense nerves." Such overkill of language makes us doubt the fact. "In order to *initiate* the new project, many *prerequisite* steps had to be planned and carried out." The writer here should be initiated into language so that he could simply "start" a project by "carrying out his careful plans." "To maintain mental *equilibrium* one must be able to *react* properly to emotions like anger or fear." For my "sanity," I'd like to "control" my emotions of anger and fear—if it is indeed one's own emotions this confusing sentence refers to.

Workbooks, with blanks to fill in from words listed at the bottom of the page, imitate objective tests. The workbooks, often clumsy in their language, are all too common in grade and high schools. Before tests and texts came up with lists and blanks to fill in, a student's vocabulary grew through exposure to correct example and pleasing usage. This exposure began in the earliest grades. Such was the case through the nineteenth century and into the twentieth century. Noah Webster's *Elementary Spelling Book,* first published in 1783, took hold in the nineteenth century, and became the prevailing word-building book in American schools even into the early 1900s. It used language in a way a test never can. Its sentences did not attempt to overwhelm the reader; they simply defined words in as precise a context as possible. Its sentences were built by ear and mind. In Webster's *Speller* of 1880, the new words were listed without definition at the top of the page, but explained by exact use in graceful sentences. The new word is self-evident—and self-explanatory —in sentences such as these.

Strong drink will debase a man.
Hard shells incase clams and oysters.
Men inflate balloons with gas, which is lighter than common
   air.
Teachers like to see their pupils polite to each other.
Idle men often delay till to-morrow things that should be done
   to-day.
Good men obey the laws of God.
I love to survey the starry heavens.
Careless girls mislay their things.
The fowler decoys the birds into his net.

Bats devour rats and mice.
The adroit rope-dancer can leap and jump and perform as
many exploits as a monkey.
Wise men employ their time in doing good to all around them.
In the time of war, merchant vessels sometimes have a convoy
　of ships of war.
Kings are men of high renown,
　Who fight and strive, to wear a crown.
God created the heavens and the earth in six days, and all that
　was made was very good.
To purloin is to steal.

Though some of these sentences reflect nineteenth-century
morality, or religious beliefs, they not only reinforce good
behavior but also have within them sustaining interest.
"Good men obey the laws of God"—a fine sentence illustrat-
ing the use of "obey"—might offend some people today, but
wouldn't necessarily throw a modern child. In the conversation of children, God often is a subject of serious talk. How
earnest six- and seven-year-olds are when discussing whether
there is a God or not. God goes secular in the statement that
"wise men" do "good to all around them." But such sentences are far more than preachment. They engage a child's
interest because bad men lurk between the lines; because the
sentences themselves suggest conflict.

Six of the above sixteen sentences describe scientific or
real-world facts. All of them succeed in expressing a precise
meaning, and are enforced by pleasing and appropriate
sound. "Hard shells incase clams and oysters" drives home
its truth by the assonance of the _l, s,_ and _a_ sounds. Whatever
the sentences, they reflect belief in the fact or the morality
stated. The anonymous composers of these sentences knew
what they were saying. In trying to "test" the student end-
lessly the sentences become his adversary.

The test tanks dominating our educational system may be
able to justify tests in mathematics, or convince us that they
can gauge reading retention, but they shouldn't be allowed
to sap the strength from our language with objective tests in

writing. If we are given another generation of tests, writing will become a rare art. The responsibility for salvaging writing falls to the American university, which instituted the objective tests for college admission twenty-five years ago, and sanctioned their use throughout the school system.

The test system and the illiteracy it has bred are the result of American faith—blind as always—in technology. Now that the ill effects of that technology are being felt on literacy and language, the educational leadership must take control. Let it claim, as an excuse, the kind of innocence that led technologists into thinking the Vietnam war could be won. But so far, the university is barely responding to the problem. It is only now *suggesting* that students be required to write throughout high school. Harvard, for instance, asks that its applicants have at least three years of secondary school writing. Hopeful Harvard applicants will comply—and Harvard will protect the literacy of its students. But by giving their seal of approval to the objective tests by requiring the SAT for admission, the universities have issued a poison the rest of America must swallow.

The antidote is to restore writing requirements on college entrance exams. But the task is formidable: ETS has a vested interest in protecting its contracts; it is marshalling every "social science" argument it can in defense of existing tests, and challenging the "scoring reliability" of essay tests.* Justifying the multiple choice approach, ETS declares that "students who recognize the problems in the writing of others are likely not to have those problems in their essays, an assumption confirmed by careful research." English teachers know this is often not the case. But the more important point is ignored by ETS: multiple choice tests do not show the student's ability to organize or interpret material in coherent writing. ETS throws up its hands at the cost of grading written exams; but surely a way exists to pay readers to read written essays; the money could be made available by cancelling ETS contracts.

*Could grades given by individual readers be any less reliable than scores given by ETS? Hardly: ETS admits to a "standard error" of 32 to 50 points on its SAT scores.

Since reading does come before writing, since the language read affects the language used by a student, since reading can make writing seem important or dull, let's look at the way reading ability is measured. In elementary school a child is measured over and over for his "grade level" in reading. To prepare the student for such tests, special texts have been developed to teach reading. Since the tests measure only retention of facts, the new readers are purely informational. Until the tests were introduced, children—once they had mastered sounds and basic words—learned to read by actually reading well-told stories. The new, "scientific" reading instruction has taken depth, meaning, and content out of reading; even narrative has been diminished. Story, with its infallible device of involving children in language by engaging them in conflict, is sacrificed to fact. The beginning reader has no real reason to read—other than the requirement to answer questions. When the fact-finding texts and tests introduce a child to the written word, their weak language gives writing a bad reputation.

In requiring endless reading for information the texts and tests not only ask for an unlikely response but for an inhuman one. Emerson, in his American Scholar Address of 1837, knew what today's reading instruction has not grasped: "Books are the best of things, well used; abused, among the worst. What is the right use? What is the one end which all means go to effect? They are for nothing but to inspire. I had better never see a book than to be warped by its attraction clean out of my own orbit." The reading texts don't recognize that the child has any orbit; they emphasize technique, yank him from fact to fact, and leave him with nothing to remember and much to dislike about reading. As Emerson wrote, "One must be an inventor to read well. As the proverb says, 'He that would bring home the wealth of the Indies, must carry out the wealth of the Indies.' There is then creative reading, as well as creative writing." Like the grammar and verbal tests, reading instruction assumes the whole world is external—a heaven arrayed with facts and it judges as cloudy the child who may have stars shining in his mind.

One technique of reading instruction is called "word at-tack." This is a method of taking language apart, like the motor of a car, in order to make it work better. Under this method, "reading" is broken up into separate skills, such as Getting the Main Idea, Using the Context, Locating the Answer, Getting the Facts, Following Directions, Working with Sounds, and Drawing Conclusions. Going further, some reading instruction addresses itself to the "Nine Components of Comprehension," component by component, cog by cog. But the objective approaches—text married to test—do not encourage comprehension. Students are mercilessly driven to find "the main idea" in one short passage after another, when no "main" or meaningful idea is given.

As an example of the language loss in the second half of the twentieth century, let us compare a passage from a widely used elementary reader, the *Merrill Linguistic Reader,* with one from an elementary reader used widely a century ago. Both passages, for beginners, deal with dogs and children. The very name of a book for six-year-olds—*Linguistic Reader*—bears the stamp of pseudoscience and predicts the absence of art in the text. Not only sound but also sense is lost in this passage from the *Linguistic Reader:*

> A rag is on Nat's mat.
> Nat looks at the rag.
> Is it a rat?
>
> He hits and hits the rag.
> He bats it to bits.
>
> A bit lit on Rags.
> Rags hit it and ran.
> Dad had to look for Rags.
>
> Rags is sad.
> Dad pats Rags.

The passage plays heavily with "phonics." But the sound is cacophonic and the sense absurd. The "Nat" who is looking at the rhyming "mat" turns out to be a boy, though through normal association one might expect a mat-owner to be a dog. Except in the exclusive world of "phonics," what sane boy would mistake a "rag" for a "rat"? Phonics that makes sense or reaches deep employs sounds that complement, rather than assault, one another. How "a bit lit on Rags" and how "Rags hit it and ran" are beyond comprehension. If the story made any sense, it might come up with a pleasing rather than a harsh pattern of sound. Some human conviction would be involved.

To return to a saner century of teaching, compare the above passage with one from *McGuffey's First Reader*, 1879, in which a girl and a dog are engaged in an illustrated chase. Tamed by a sensible incident, the phonics results in pleasing sound. Though most early readers do better than Nat, mat, and Rags, the craze for "phonics" on one hand and fact on the other makes even this McGuffey episode seem a lost art:

> See Rab! See Ann!
> See! Rab has the hat.
> Can Ann catch Rab?
> Ann can catch Rab.
> See! She has the hat.
> Now Ann can pat Rab.
> Let me pat Rab, too.

The objective tests, and the reading texts they inspire, come from a laboratory mentality lacking art and humanity. Bent on dissection, this kind of education lacks coherence, and addresses itself at best to particular brain cells, never to the whole creature. Art, at the level of simplicity as well as complexity, is the voice of mind and spirit working together in the individual. Happily, many teachers resist the fragmented approach of technology. Many contemporary children's books still engage the child's ear by their language and poetic conflict, as traditional fairy tales do. But in the educational lab, spirit is a dirty word, a germ; the mental game is antiseptic. Perhaps the educational technologists take care of their spirit in their leisure time, by going to concerts. Schools that send students from dreary workbooks to free-form art classes suffer the same split personality. Creativity and discipline need to be merged in every humanistic undertaking; one cannot exist without the other.

It is only since the technology of reading instruction has taken hold in schools that America has had a noticeable reading problem. After a generation of technological teaching, the nation confronts a problem that the mechanical approach of text and test has fostered.

"As a teacher of fifth-grade students for more than ten years," a New York City public school teacher recently wrote *The New York Times*, "I can vouch for the invalidity of these horrendous tests. Many a poor reader has tested too high through random guess work, and many a good reader has tested poorly because he or she was nervous, had a headache that morning or his or her answer was better than the 'correct' one. The cost of these test booklets is well over $1 million, not including the valuable teaching hours wasted on administering and computing these useless papers. These invalid scores, by the way, are entered on the child's permanent records, and the student is often tracked in junior high school on the basis of these tests." In many public schools an automatic 10 percent of six-year-olds are labeled—often for the rest of their school years—as having "learning disabilities." Today it is almost common for a child to have a reading problem. American educators have turned their work over to technologists who, isolated in their specialization, innocent of literature, contemptuous of history, but bedazzled by technique, do not know how to teach. The science these technologists have sold the schools is disabled. They, not the young people who cannot read adequately, are responsible for the growth of the reading problem.

A century ago the main problem in schools was truancy; but if a child stayed in school, he did learn to read and write. The six-volume *McGuffey's Reader*, the dominant American schoolbook through the nineteenth and into the twentieth century, poured out little melodramas in short passages pleasing to a child's ear and mind. Because many of the tales, written by schoolteachers, were morality tales, they necessarily presented the stark conflict of melodrama. Conflict—as all other ages but ours have known—is the point of interest on which a child can concentrate. The books accomplished their main purpose—teaching people to read—with an absolute precision of language. The style, necessarily slow for early readers, crisper for older children, was simplicity itself. The language, pleasing to hear as well as remarkably clear, influenced the way in which Americans wrote.

Successor to the dour and moralistic New England primers of the eighteenth century, the *McGuffy Readers* portrayed the realities of human nature even while preaching a moral code. In one story from *McGuffey's Second Reader* (editions of 1879, 1896, 1907, 1920), a big and little brother carry either end of a pole on which a bag of things for grandmother is hung. The older brother is tempted to shift the burden toward his brother's side: "If I slip the basket near him, his side will be heavy and mine light; but if the basket is in the middle of the pole, it will be as heavy for me as for him. Tom does not know this as I do." Deciding not to "do what is wrong," but instead, slipping the basket "quite near his own end," he carries the heavier burden and is happy because he has not "deceived his brother." Such conflict not only teaches fairness but also engages a child's interest because of what we call sibling rivalry.

This short poem, with conflict underlying its truth, delights my seven-year-old son:

> Work while you work,
>   Play while you play,
> One thing each time,
>   That is the way.
>
> All that you do,
>   Do with your might,
> Things done by halves,
>   Are not done right.

Creating melodrama out of misfortune, the tales solved the latter by a combination of self-help and sympathy. "Poor Davy had no father, and his mother had to work hard to keep him at school." Stung by his schoolmates' "cruel words" about his "ragged clothes," he mopes in the woods until his teacher, finding him there, comes up with a plan to help him. " 'Oh, what is it?' he said, sitting up with a look of hope." Helping him gather and arrange "the prettiest flowers, and the most dainty ferns and mosses," she sends him into the nearby city to be a "little flower merchant." He "soon earned enough money to buy new clothes."

The tales, referring frequently to poverty and showing sympathy with the poor, edge into social conscience. In the *Third Reader,* a city boy longs to buy "some pretty books" with "two bright, new silver dollars" his father gives him as a New Year's gift. On the snowy street he sees a "poor German family, the father, mother, and three children shivering with cold." Not understanding the boy's New Year's greeting, the immigrant "pointed to his mouth, and to the children, as if to say, 'These little ones have had nothing to eat for a long time.' Edward quickly understood that these poor people were in distress. He took out his dollars, and gave one to the man, and the other to his wife." A child's poem in *McGuffey's Third Reader* exemplifies the pervasive theme of brotherhood that runs through the *Readers*. It echoes a lyric now found in *The Threepenny Opera.*

> Lend a hand to one another
> In the daily toil of life;
> When we meet a weaker brother,
> Let us help him in the strife.
> There is none so rich but may
> In his turn, be forced to borrow;
> And the poor man's lot to-day
> May become our own to-morrow.
>
> Lend a hand to one another:
> When malicious tongues have thrown
> Dark suspicion on your brother.

Be not prompt to cast a stone.
There is none so good but may
Run adrift in shame and sorrow.
And the good man of to-day
May become the bad to-morrow.

Lend a hand to one another:
In the race for Honor's crown;
Should it fall upon your brother,
Let not envy tear it down.
Lend a hand to all, we pray,
In their sunshine or their sorrow;
And the prize they've won today
May become our own tomorrow.

McGuffey's—and the similar readers and primers used into this century—took their ethics from the Judeo-Christian tradition and made them secular. Engaging the child's attention in conflict, the nineteenth-century readers taught civic and social virtue in the conflict's resolution. How pallid are the informational passages in today's readers beside them. In one of today's better readers is this typical conflict: Two boys (black and white) frighten two girls (black and white) with a toy frog; the girls retaliate by letting a live frog loose in the boys' tent. Where stories in contemporary readers do engage in conflict, they don't reach very far into human experience; like children's television, they try to excite. When the old readers worked with the child's deepest feelings of pity and fear, they sought to educate his character for life in a democratic society. Certainly not designed to prepare a society for change and reform, the readers nevertheless reflected ethics that made change and reform possible. Behind the assimilation of immigrant generations, the reform of monopoly, the recognition of the rights of the working man in the early twentieth century lay the good work of McGuffey.

Sometimes catering to self-interest—by rewarding good behavior with love, success, or silver dollars—the tales nevertheless made the little characters work hard to be good. Some of the scenes, in their melodrama and pity for the poor, are almost Chaplinesque. The influence of McGuffey on a generation of writers can be understood as an influence on many. Such a cynic as H. L. Mencken, looking back on his own education in the 1890s, could deride the evangelistic "blah in the McGuffey Readers and penmanship copy books," but, confronting in the 1920s "a new and complicated science" in education, "driving the [school] ma'ams crazy, and converting the children into laboratory animals," he favors "the old singsong system. . . . One could grasp . . . without graphs." (Part of McGuffey's success in teaching reading was undoubtedly group recitation. New words at the head of each entry were sounded aloud by a whole class. Since children do learn from imitation of each other, teaching that leaves group work out in favor of "individual attention" may omit a crucial aspect of learning.) Morality was —and is—something a child can grasp. Even in today's secular society, moral concern is a child's natural domain, not because children are good, but because the moral tale acknowledges a struggle between good and evil, a struggle that a child, in his polar opposites of self-interest and need for others, understands. Searching for heroes and heroines, pitting the good guys against the bad, children still search for stark opposites—for the good witch and the wicked. Tales with a clear moral are effective teachers of reading. Though they have now come back into print, *McGuffey's Readers* were dropped in the wake of change following World War I. One reason, no doubt, for Mencken and for others, was their hypocrisy. The world was not the pretty place of concern for others that McGuffey described. The world may have been hypocritical, but the *Readers* sought values. While some teachers may have been "hypocrites," the texts were able to teach democratic virtue by recognizing that a child's fear for himself could be transformed into sympathy for others. While the *Readers* could evoke, as in Mencken's first assault, howls of derision, they did teach a decent use of language and built character at the same time.

Some of today's reading texts try to engage the child's interest by sociological relevance. The relevant story presents an integrated picture of American life—black and white, in pictures and text—but often hasn't much of a story to tell. A black child can benefit, no doubt, from stories about black people, as can white children, if the story has depth. If the text talks only street talk and rent strikes, it won't help language. Langston Hughes' "Ballad of the Landlord," dramatizing the conflict between landlord and tenant, will engage any child by its inherent conflict—and thus will teach something. Literature can teach by reason of its tension and poetry, but relevance and tests cannot. Melodrama, which reaches deep into a child's fears and hopes, is a better teacher than sociological truisms.

In "the return to basics" movement, *McGuffey's Readers* are again being used in a few schools. At the Pilgrim School, attached to a Congregational church in Los Angeles, teachers once skeptical of *McGuffey's* now praise its effect. "When children leave kindergarten, they read," says one teacher who objected to using it when she began ten years ago; now she claims that the first graders can spell "Cincinnati," "centipede," and "telephone." Half of the school's enrollment comes from minority groups—but the nonwhite children have reportedly done well with the text. Astutely perhaps, the teachers were bothered by the absence of minority representation in the texts before they began using them. The use of *McGuffey's Readers* is one example of how schools can withstand the technological age—and create worlds of learning apart from it, in defiance of it. *Dick and Jane,* the successors to the *Readers* in the thirties and forties, are pale by comparison.

Offering more than melodrama and morality, the *Readers* have in the passage of time become myth. In their open-air settings, in their fields, woods, and ponds—in their children, parents, grandparents—the stories become a mythology of American life at a time when in reality it had, for the lucky, reached a point of coherence. Hypocrisy needs always to be thrown out. But hypocrisy in one age may become myth in another.

Teaching Open Admissions students, I have found that some respond quickly to reading, others are sluggish—but all respond to reading that inspires them. To my chagrin, I've even found some students failing to understand the most sublime subtleties that other students have produced in their writing. Teaching writing, I have sought to awaken students to meaning and to imagery. But after twelve years of numbing reading instruction in schools, a sensitive response to prose and poetry is not to be expected. After all, some schools are graduating twelfth graders with eighth-grade reading ability.

The alarmed citizenry should know the content of the tests that determine an "eighth grade" level. The Cooperative English Test in Reading Comprehension—from the same test tank that produces the SAT, TSWE, and English Achievement Tests—represents the tests that high school students are trained for and stuck with. It is used across the nation to determine a "national norm" for college reading. In New York City, at least four of the City University's senior colleges use it to gauge reading ability and to place students in remedial courses.

Let's see what the test contains. To many poor and minority students the test may seem foreign. Of the thirteen passages on a recent test, one has as its setting a tennis court on a country estate; a second uses gourmet cooking and symphonic concerts to make its recherché point; a third is all about undergraduate life at Cambridge University; a fourth is concerned with the daily habits of nineteenth-century British literati. Other topics were not class-related: a passage on the French Revolution, one on the nineteenth-century plow, three on the animal kingdom, two on the sale of jewelry, and one on Arab history. But not one passage is about current or recent events, or American history, literature, or life.

Since the young from the Bronx and Dixie, the Rockies and Grand Rapids, have to wade through it, here is the country-estate passage:

Most boys at school have at some time learned the dates of the English kings. But as a rule they fail to keep this up and lose all the good of it. I have an old friend, a college classmate, who has carefully kept this knowledge alive. He is now able in his old age to get great enjoyment from saying these dates to himself. His keepers tell me that he shows many other signs of mental activity and often recites for them lists of genitive plurals and verbs that take the dative.

It pleased me, I must say, at my country place last summer when there was some mathematical difficulty about marking the tennis court to have one of my guests, a student in my classes at Yale, offer to work out the measurements with a logarithm. He said it was quite simple. He needed, in short, nothing but a hypotenuse and two acute angles, all of which luckily were found around the place. It was very interesting to watch the boy calculate, at first. I am certain he would have gotten the solution, only while he was preparing to mark the courts by means of his logarithm the chauffeur marked it with whitewash.

Of the six questions on the passage, three are straightforward and offer one clear-cut answer out of four possibilities. The only possible answer to a fourth question requires the student to agree that the old man was "in a mental institution." But surely the old man, sounding more senile than psychotic, is merely in an old people's home. A fifth question asks for the one place in the passage where the writer "introduces a little humor." But he is sly throughout the passage. The test makers, as always, are not discerning. A sixth question is a prize example of the ambiguity the tests engage in and the confusion they spread to the young.

> The main point of the passage is that
> E. many useless things are learned at school.
> F. memorizing damages the brain.
> G. dates are sometimes useful.
> H. mathematics is helpful in practical situations.

There is no "main point" to a passage that engages, above all else, in paradox. Dates are certainly useful to the old man —though the test makers might deny it—simply because they give him pleasure. But that answer (*G*) is only a "main point" of the first paragraph. Mathematics is not helpful to the young man in this situation (*H*). Certainly the passage doesn't tell us heresy—that many useless things are learned at school (*E*). As in so many of the tests, there is no "right" answer—only obscurity.

In another passage, about the intense pleasure of a first experience, a student has to grasp a series of upper-class titillations. "One's first *Filet Mignon Béarnaise* is a ravishment. The second, unless it occurs after an interval of repose, is less effective." A colleague of mine, forced to administer the test, was so upset by the question that she seized the microphone to explain what *Filet Mignon Béarnaise* was. The passage concludes: "When next you see me tiptoeing out of a concert and inquire anxiously, 'What! Aren't you staying for the Pathétique?' you will hear me whisper, 'No thanks, I'm on the wagon.' " Neither a knowledge of Beethoven nor an effete view of experience is necessary for either college or reading. Cherish it as some may, the idiom "on the wagon" is as much a class idiom as *Béarnaise* sauce. Thrown by his ignorance of French cuisine and of middle-class slang, a black student or a midwesterner who can read and think perfectly well might not be able to answer the questions. Or just put off by the foolishness of the test, he could take his resentment out on all reading.

No other country, civilized or uncivilized, has delivered its students to the objective-test factory. European democracies still have the sense to require written exams to their universities. But in America objective tests are big money. ETS, a nonprofit educational organization that grossed $80 million last year, supervises more than 300 testing programs. Aside from the SAT, ETS gives the SSAT (Secondary School Admission Test), the LSAT (Law School Admission Test), and the Graduate Record Examination (also a multiple choice test used for graduate school admission). ETS supplies public schools with its Step Test and its Basic Skills Achievement Test, but the bulk of the school tests come from private corporations. Among the widely used school tests are McGraw Hill's California Test of Basic Skills, the Psychological Corporation's Stanford Achievement Test, the Iowa Test Bureau's Test of Basic Skills. Add to these not only the reading texts but also the test-inspired workbooks, with objective questions in the "language arts," and the dreary aspects of American schooling come clear. With objective tests at every level of education, is it any wonder that writing has been ignored?

No critic has defined the shortcomings of the SAT better than Ralph Nader. "ETS has us all locked into a test that doesn't look for creativity, stamina, motivation, or ethics— which are the four qualities on which man's greatest achievements are based." Our mania for measurement, our naïve assumption that we will discover a true meritocracy through objective standards, contradicts the original American idea. When Jefferson wrote of a "natural aristocracy" emerging from an elementary and then a "higher degree" of education in preparation for the university, he thought that "worth and genius would thus have been sought from every condition of life." "Virtue and talent" were to be relentlessly encouraged and sought in schools at all levels. What worth, what talent, what virtue, does objective testing measure? Rather than rewarding visible intellectual work done in the classroom, the tests reward a cleverness that even the clever can doubt.

Though ETS announces that the SAT is not designed to judge the "worth" of anyone, the tests set implicit standards of worth by becoming a passport to education, income, and social status. An SAT score—the score on a single test—can set the direction of a lifetime. Though there is increasing skepticism about the SAT, the score can still weigh heavily. If a college has an adequate admissions staff, it can afford to consider other factors. But the many colleges that have small staffs must rely heavily on SAT numbers. ETS admits that a 66-point difference in verbal scores is statistically meaningless.* Yet a 66-point difference between two students can mean that one will get into a particular college while the other will be denied admission. Surely the SAT, both because of the statistical problem and the importance of the score on a single test, stirs resentment among the young. Students spend valuable classroom hours in the crash courses—and even attend summer school—to "learn" to take the test. Though the coaching sessions can be helpful, they also teach an appropriate cynicism toward "the system." Substantial education—the history of man or nation—is set aside in order to beat the test. The test is "the system," to be overcome by studying vocabulary lists, by taking practice tests, by learning the technique of test taking. Resentment and cynicism are two lessons taught by the American way of testing.

A student who hasn't had to write in school, who has suffered objective education or just neglect, must first discover, however unconsciously, an identity. He must act on that identity through language. In their wide embrace the tests, as a matter of course, squeeze and stifle identity. The student may not be aware that his own mind is the source of expression—in school he has stopped using it. To learn to write, students have to recover from the fear of the written word that education has left them with; and to teach writing, teachers must help in that recovery, must try to reach the mind and restore it to use. Grammar is learned neither from the tests nor from grammar books, but from the risk of writing.

The students quoted in this book, shunted aside by objective tests and placed in other classes that gave them more objective tests and stupefying drills, began by writing from experience. Because many are black or Puerto Rican, many have come from ghetto schools where barely any writing was

*The 66-point difference is meaningless because 66 points could have been attained by such external factors as guesswork.

asked of them. Enrolled either as SEEK or Open Admissions students, they have been in classes of mine at Brooklyn College, or at York College, both four-year colleges of the City University of New York. The poor have responded to the same approach I've used with the better-off, the black to the same approach as the white. It has been said that methods used to teach minority students are now being used to teach the illiterate middle class; that's true, but my approach hasn't been tailored to any one group. It grew out of a feeling about what the human voice can do—and was based on my background as a writer. Black or white, poor or middle class, the students here have responded. The fearful have gained courage. Those who didn't learn to write weren't "dumb," but so pinched by circumstances in mind and emotions that their courage for writing had failed. Those who have broken through to clarity and coherence have had to master the particulars of standard American grammar through their own correction, through workbook exercises, through classroom instruction. Learning standard American grammar has been a problem for whites as well as blacks, but once the self is at stake—once writing matters—students find reason to honor the language.

Some of the most compelling writing has come from using the senses. Asked to bring their sight, hearing, and smell into play, students have written well before embarking on tougher assignments. A student so inarticulate that I could never get much conversation out of him, reticent because of what I could only guess were the emotional problems of poverty, wrote this in class.

I am watching a large hawk soaring in the sky like a stringless kite. Perhaps this massive bird is hunting but it looks as though it is just relaxing while flying with much grace. The bird reminds me of one of those soundless gliding planes floating in the sky without an engine. I can see the bird circling and changing elevation with just a twitch of his tail, flying smooth without ever flapping it's huge extended wings. There is a slight hush in the fields and woods when the bird is around. It seems that all other wildlife notes the hawk's presence and camouflages themselves by lying motionless, waiting for the large dark shadow in the clear sky to depart. These birds are true leaders of the sky.

The boy, tall, solemn, nicely mannered, never "tested" well. Getting him to write regularly was difficult, though at the end of the course he came to life and participated more. A student who tested well might have lost language and perceptions on the way to his scores; in writing, would he see a bird "circling and changing elevation with just a twitch of his tail"?

On a rainy Saturday in a review class, another student wrote of the rain: "When it rains, in my mind's eye it looks like sheets of sandpaper coming down from a colorless sky. When I go out into it, once the droplets hit my face, it feels like a thousand spear tips giving every pore a moment of pleasure or pain. But above all the rain is the lack of movement in which I cannot escape." When I saw him the next year, walking along the street with stooped shoulders, he said he was still working on his writing. Why are students who show such patterns of sound and metaphor in their writing failing? A strong case can be made for blaming it on rules-and-regulations teaching, and poverty and its attendant problems.

A black girl who would find verbal pairs ridiculous, who would surely leave all the test blanks blank, who would be declared "educationally deprived," if not a dummy, brought definition to "Soul," a word that would baffle a test maker, in an in-class assignment:

> Soul cannot be defined or explained. Soul is felt; soul is.
> The voice of Aretha or Roberta Flack is Soul genuine, clear, true blue Soul. In the corn bread, collard greens and hamhocks you had for dinner, you get that Soul. The flavor. It's that fast talkin', slow boppin' Dude on the corner trying to run his game. It's a mother and her beautiful black baby playing. It's that chicken on Sunday and the hymn your mother hums in the kitchen. It's that jazzy musician's horn.

It's in every black man's heart waiting to be uncovered. It's profound beauty and a magical wonder. All these things combine to make up Soul.

The student wrote this in the second of three remedial courses offered at the school. She had reached into her culture. In several minutes, she had made a "synthesis." In a subjective exercise, full of feeling, she was able to unite popular music and old old hymns, mothers with children, and numbers men on the street. She didn't talk much in class, but her writing was eloquent. In class she sat still and stared straight ahead, as though she were looking way beyond the classroom. The next term she completed the final remedial course, and wrote a successful term paper.

One white student was in that all-black class. He wrote a paper defining the word "spirit." That was a tactful, though probably unnecessary translation I made of "soul" into an idiom he might feel comfortable with. His first attempts at writing were clumsy. But he had begun to come up with lyric phrases amid the confusion. He was becoming very much himself.

Spirit is the undiscovered fluid that flows through you when a smile rises or you offer a helping hand. It's being you and being proud of it. No one can buy it or force it on themselves, it comes naturally. The world becomes colorful, a playground for life, not just yours, but others'. It's a utopia within the person himself.

He, too, had personal problems, one of which was low self-esteem. Like most CUNY students, he lived at home with his parents, and he was trying to break away from them. "I don't spend my weekends at home anymore," he explained. His father, he said, was an "Archie Bunker" type. To the blacks in the class, Archie Bunker was a fool made public and *All in the Family* an enjoyable satire. Wearing a habitual lumberjacket, this student was not at all inhibited by being a minority in the class, in fact, the openness of the black students was perhaps a liberating influence for him.

CARNEGIE LIBRARY
LIVINGSTONE COLLEGE
SALISBURY, N. C. 28144

Like so many Open Admissions students, he grew in college. As he wrote, he gained self-confidence. When I encountered him a year later, he seemed to have grown physically; he had passed the third remedial course, and he wore an easy smile.

Some black students in the class had more difficult family problems than he, but they normally didn't talk about them. Sometimes, however, the family situation became clear in their writing. In their conversations with me about themselves, they were guarded; and I didn't pry. Writing classes need to be a therapy for all sorts of numbness, and I was the unlicensed practitioner. I urge them to be somebody in their writing. They get the idea that I respect them. Writing is one of the ways the individual speaks. It is a significant act. They often hear me say: *In this class of fifteen students there should be fifteen different papers on the same subject. There are fifteen different individuals here. If you don't think you're important, you won't write. Writing is honoring yourself, your experience, your point of view, your individuality.* With exhortation after exhortation, punch after punch, I have found that good writing begins to come in; work goes forward on particular writing problems. Sometimes a student persists in turning in stilted, undeveloped papers. Then I have to face him or her with firm, but honest criticism. I am upset because the student cannot find his identity in writing. I tell the student he is trying to imitate some poorly written textbook, that he is trying to impress me, but is only making himself look ridiculous. In such a face-to-face conversation comes a tense moment. But four times out of five the next paper is infinitely better. The rewards, for the student and for me, are significant.

Reading—if it involves the student—introduces him to language and helps in his writing. But he must be able to respond to the book. One hopes the student will be influenced by good writers, and learn how to organize ideas. Essays, like any other kind of writing, depend for their final effectiveness on organization. Organization comes not from formula but from purpose. The separate parts of a paper are drawn together by the magnet of vision. A paper begins, not with an introduction, but with the strongest thought in the writer's mind. Thought breeds thought. "To produce a mighty book," wrote Melville, "you must choose a mighty theme." How does a writer find a purpose except by drumming it out of himself? He can never know what the related parts of a paper are unless he is aware, somehow, in some way, of the intricate relationships of his own impulses and tensions. To write, one must be introspective—a quality that objective tests try to rub out. To write a book report, a student must not only be familiar with the book, but also able to react to it. Without that ability the writer cannot begin to write: he doesn't know what to emphasize or omit; he doesn't know how to interpret what he has read. The student who can't react to the book usually turns in a plot summary. To be able to react to an assigned topic, the writer must first be able to sort out the world he knows and then relate it to the topic; if he can't organize that, he will have difficulty responding to a world someone else has created in a book. Learning to write, then, necessarily begins with writing from experience and observation. Then it must be connected with the experience of others. There are no formulas for thinking.

But English instructors still try to provide formulas. *Every paragraph must have a topic sentence. Where is your topic sentence?* Students in search of the topic sentence don't have the opportunity to think. To get students to write is to get them to think. Objective education, whether by tests or the teaching of rules, denies this and reaps the unfortunate results.

Some academics dismiss "creative writing" as unsuitable for composition courses. I've found few students at this stage ready or able to write any but the most suffocating kind of fiction. But a dislike of creative writing can inhibit teachers from asking for an imaginative rendering of experience. Some teachers might think the following paper "creative," but it was not "made up." It was reality interpreted and embellished. Embellishment, required in all sorts of writing, always requires a creative energy.

The Shooting Gallery

He had a bad night selling everything he stole for practically nothing. Having enough money for one good fix would keep him together another day. After running the three blocks he sees his man and cops.

Making his way up the rickety stairs, two at a time, and down the long dark hallway, he says the magic words and enters the sparsely furnished shabby apartment called the "Shooting Gallery." Sitting on the floor along the grimy, spotted wall and in a dirty corner are a few familiar faces unaware of his presence. They are worlds away. A gripping pain hits him in the pit of his stomach as he waits for a set of works and curses himself for not having his own. Impatiently he yells, "Come on man, hurry up!" to a fellow junkie in the process of shooting up. He dumps the white powder into a spoon, adds a few drops of water and holding a flame beneath it, begins to cook the meal his body is craving.

All along his arms are black track marks and open puss-filled sores. As he ties his arm off just above the elbow with a belt, he grimaces at the thought of the pain he is about to feel when he uses the back of his hand. He balls up a tight hand and misses. "Damnit," he thinks. His body is tense as he wiggles the spike around under his skin in search of the vein. Wincing, he hits home and is relieved at the sight of the red fluid entering the small glass tube. With a sigh he unloosens the tie and slowly squeezes the rubber tip until all the milky liquid disappears into his hand which almost immediately puffs up like a balloon.

The sweat pours down his face like water and his body relaxes as his expression changes from tense craving to peaceful satisfaction. Mouth open, eyes closed and head bent, he nods his way into his very own world. Unaware of the saliva dripping from the corner of his mouth, he grooves for hours. He's safe until reality invades his world, safe to start all over again.

This piece, stunning in its form and honesty, was written by a copper-skinned girl in her twenties, who often mounted a braid in a perfect oval at the top of her head. The assignment was to write a description of a person real or imaginary living in New York. Without ever hearing the hideous words *topic sentence,* the writer had formed her idea in concise language—"begins to cook the meal his body is craving." In class we had been talking about the judgment the writer must exercise in order to eliminate deadwood, to put secondary matters in a secondary place, to let sentences climb to importance at the end. In three or four drafts she had written the paper, "boiling it down" all along, she said, taking out the unessential, building up the truth. I'm sure she had reading in her head—but not the kind the tests ask for. Her ear and her eye had been tuned to the world, verbal, visual, hidden. I suspect she was more of a writer than a reader; she had kept a journal of impressions, she allowed, over a period of time. Her vocabulary was small, but still she could write. A few days later, when we were reading a column by Tom Wicker in *The New York Times*—as an example of writing—she asked what the words "expedient" and "artifice" meant.

Once, when I casually asked her where she had been after she had been absent a few days, a doleful young man in the class piped up, "She's getting married." And sure of her target, uninhibited about herself, she let forth, "I'm not getting married. I'm trying to get divorced." Directness is often the advantage of the disadvantaged. And rather than give them a new language to write in, or prove their disability through tests, I encourage that directness. The same young man who had taunted her had turned in a disorganized paper on Spanish Harlem, his own neighborhood. His writing was sporadic and virtually hopeless. But in a class discussion over the malfeasances of Vice President Agnew, he got mad and, asked to write his thoughts down, turned in a paragraph with the only unity I ever saw in his writing. "Frank," I exclaimed, "that has unity." "That's not unity," he yelled back. "That's anger."

He had inadvertently hit on a truth. The emotional response to a subject forces language into a pattern. Emotions color the words and speed the style. What T. S. Eliot called "squads of undisciplined emotion" must have a captain. But the force in charge is not mind alone. Some higher power—emerging from mind and emotion together—musters a point of view, a purpose, and puts both mind and emotion to work.

3 Educations

When, in 1970, I was being interviewed for the SEEK job at York, a blunt black lady counselor, who had studied my résumé, asked what someone raised in Fairfield County, Connecticut, could know about urban kids. I couldn't tell her what I knew, but said that Stamford was not all lawns; it was an industrial city as well.

But in one way the black lady interviewer was right. Like most white people who grew up liberal in a northern environment, I had never known many blacks. The one black whom I had known and admired was Moses Davis, an elegant gentleman who ran my parents' home in the last ten years of my mother's life. My mother, southern by birth, had overcome the traditional prejudices in her years in the North, but maintained a little of her accent and much of her culture. She and Moses Davis were like kin. I used to be a bit embarrassed by the relationship—and embarrassed by my embarrassment. "The Madam," he called her. Though she called him "Moses," she would behold him with the same smile she held for others she loved and respected. They regarded each other as persons.

Finding the South, which he loved, good enough only to visit, Moses Davis had come North and made a business out of running households, which he did with style as well as mystery. "You just keep on tryin', Miss Carol," he told my wife after he had tasted a slice of the first cake she had ever baked. "You just keep on tryin'." He had kept his identity intact. When the tension between generations comes up in my classes—a girl once said that her mother wasn't "black, but colored"—I think of him. To make the best of what our time has given us is a triumph.

Until I got to know my students, I fear I essentially pitied blacks. I was like the well-intentioned whites Du Bois wrote about, painfully, seventy years ago. They just "flutter around" an unasked question, but never come to it directly: "How does it feel to be a problem?" The first steps of sensitivity in any limited man may be to see a problem, not a person.

Had I, as a college freshman, been asked to write an essay on any subject of my choosing, I might not have been wordless, but I doubt I would have done as well as some of my free, unlearned students. Although I have felt the world pressing in on me, its antagonisms were but a nudge compared to what most black students have felt. If they haven't had all the spirit knocked out of them—as even some white students have had—if they are alive to both joy and contempt, they can write surprisingly well, even if they disdain school and studying. The best responses, coming from a spiral core of identity, are not one-dimensional; released on paper, they speak for a multisided mind. One of these students wrote this in the second remedial course:

Spring is busting out all over. Throughout the meadows and the hills.

Winter is gone and has done its thing. Now we can discard our shovels and plows. Goodbye winter and glad to see you spring. Spring you really kicked winter right in the ass. Three cheers for spring and let every bell ring. The little animals in the woods shout it's spring. The cows in every pasture have beautiful green grass to munch on. Children run till their

hearts beg them mercy. Construction of buildings shoot sky
high every day.

Summer, good old summer. This is the time of race riots.

"Hey, white boy, why do you always lie on the beach for
a suntan? Is it because deep down inside you know black is
beautiful."

"Hey, nigger, why don't you get your ass out of the way
of my sunlight."

A loose, powerful figure, Burton was a veritable song-
writer. The active, precise verb, the urban pastoral image,
were for him forces, part natural, part mysterious. In another
paper (the topic was "What is on your mind?") he wrote this:

Not a thing is on my mind. Not one single thing is running
through my brains. What a shame to sit in a room full of
wonderful people and think of nothing. What a shame to sit
next to a window and see foxy girls, trucks, cars, and buses
speed past.

A blank heavy head sitting on a tired neck doing nothing.
A blank heavy head with big brown eyes, a shiny nose and
a bright smile (when made to laugh), just staring into space.

Not a thing is on my mind. Time ticks away and nothing,
no nothing is running through this thick skull. What would
happen if I did think of something? Would I blow a fuse?
Would I make history?

Physically, it was a fair description. Over six feet tall,
hunched over the writing arm of his chair, he rode the chair
like the driver of a racing car. His writing had form and irony
coming out, of all detestable places, in the classroom. His
eyes widened with amusement, then narrowed with resistance. Once I saw him in the disc-jockey booth in the crowded
cafeteria, where he presided over the soul records. One day,
I happened to be sitting next to a student, my pants leg rolled
up as I sought to get at an itch. Passing by, Burton stuck his
head—and a grin—in the open window and said, "You sure
got nice legs, Mr. Wheeler." I told him as he went by that
he was not the first to think so. Though he had identity in

plentiful supply, he resisted instruction. He was a great proponent of soul, but when I asked him to write a paper defining what soul was, he dismissed the notion. He would only say that "soul was having everything together. . . . A black party has so much soul that it's completely different from a white party." He couldn't take direction, but was a master of indirection, creating out of turbulence. In a paper he was assigned to write at home he took death as his topic and described it as the greatest injustice of all time.

If I could live my life again, I would cease the dying and reincarnate the dead. None deserves to die, not a soul deserves to die.

If I could live my life again blacks and white would be totally equal to each other. Intelligence would be the prime and the most desirable matter in the universe. The days would be longer and the nights shorter. Citizens would be citizens.

When I die and if I die, let reincarnation dig me up to experiences unknown.

His irony presided over the injustices of the world in that last line, with a play on slang—"dig"—mixed with formal language. His exuberance, for all its flight, had subtlety. The day after the Muhammed Ali–Frazier fight, he brought to class a poem he had written overnight.

Cassius Clay on the floor you lay
   in the middle
   of the ring Frazier
   did his thing
Frazier knocked you out in the
   fifteenth bout and now you
   let your fans down
   you great big mouth clown
Muhammed Ali don't look at me
   I'm only the writer
   you're the former heavy weight
   fighter
Classius Clay on the floor you lay

you'll see stars
from now till the next day
Frazier really gave you a blow
but we all
        know you'll get another
        chance to do your Ali dance
When you get your chance (MAN) do
        your Ali dance and knock
        Frazier
        the King
        Clear
        Out of
        the
        ring.

Burton could handle complexities. Criticism and approval of Ali were no problem. In the word "look," the
two o's were drawn as round human eyes. The pattern of
sound and the rhyme itself, from a poet, showed emotion
playing the strings of the mind. Yet he would play his
music only at the right temperature. He was imprisoned
in subjectivity; his sensitivity set limits on what he would
and would not do. Asked to write on an assigned subject
he was familiar with—on soul, on local politics, on his
neighborhood—he would clam up. His opinions and point
of view were abundant, but popped out in the sand or the
season. Just at the time I was trying to get the class to
write about *The Great Gatsby,* he dropped out of the
course. Moving from the creative to the expository
wouldn't work for him. At least the creative got him to
write. He had passed the first remedial course at a lope,
but could not move into metaphor larger than his own
creation. I had taken *Gatsby* as a saga of America and
the corruption of a dream; Gatsby could drive a cream-
colored Cadillac on 125th Street, couldn't he? Burton
even liked the sound of Fitzgerald's closing passage,
which I read aloud. But he never read much of the book
—he turned in a paper so ill-informed I couldn't conclude

otherwise. I had hoped he would rewrite it, but he never came to class again. His exuberance had become a sulk.

I have seen resentment of authority—displaced onto books, schoolwork, discipline—often enough in gifted young black men to suspect the origins. I knew that Burton wasn't from desperate poverty, but as a black he was vulnerable to the interior diseases of racism. Although a historian has recently reported that black families exhibited stability following the Civil War and up to the 1920s—like *Roots,* this idea puts the myth of the shattered black family to sleep— I know just as well from the experience of my students that the black family in the North, bearing impossible pressures, sometimes breaks apart. But the Moynihan Report on the black family did fail to consider the way in which the extended family structure of the black family compensates for urban fractures: the man who hasn't been able to sustain his role as a husband, for example, may be the uncle helping to hold another family together. The legacy of racism—hounding the male in the South, favoring in position and protection the black woman—has its counterpart in the North, where black men can't find jobs, where boys grow up without fathers to model themselves after.

In the face of this disaster, black women, as I have seen them, are marvels to behold—raising children, going to school, bearing family and work burdens. Still, the world hasn't given them, as it has given the black male, standards all too easy to fail to meet. If women are the breadwinners, it is not because society has expected that leadership from them; they rise to it out of necessity. Black women give lip service but little fervor to the women's liberation movement, for they already have enough to worry about. A young black woman student of mine found her husband, a community college student, behaving oddly and threatening to leave home when his grades started to decline. When, at her suggestion, he came to see me, I met an intelligent, sensitive, quivering man, so overwrought about his performance that he became his own worst enemy. Months later he did leave his wife; and she carried on, finally being graduated, with her children at her side. Expectations of male leadership and performance conspire to make some men feel failure at the slightest slip. It will take a great deal more humanness—and much more opportunity—for black males to ride life more easily.

Recently, when I mentioned to a gifted but disorganized male student that he needed more discipline in his work, he shot back instantly, "I get enough of that discipline talk from my old lady. I don't want it from you." Many young black men are touching in their studiousness—and beneficiaries of parental influence, maternal and paternal. But when students balk at writing an assignment or at reading a book, I know who it is, in our society and in theirs, that tell children to study in the first place. The strong mothers in their lives become, at some point, authority figures that the children resent. Ghetto schools, often taught by women, do not offer the models most young men need. While many male students have been promising and accomplished in SEEK, black women have been consistently more successful. One young man, who worked slowly and steadily, had perception and grace in his writing. He had at first only written garbled metaphors of frustrated love. He had broken up with his girl, he explained one day, because he did not want to sire a family for which he could not take the responsibility. One year later, he saw her through the window of her apartment holding a child. She had wanted a child and had gotten pregnant by another man. The student was tormented, he told me, by the wish to become that child's father, that girl's husband—to care for them. Later, reading a Hawthorne short story, "Roger Malvern's Burial," he perceived more brightly than anyone else the moral dilemma Hawthorne had brought forth. He could work his way out of the personal into somebody else's metaphor. And, whenever students do that, they have transcended their own pain and insecurity, and climbed out of themselves into a larger world.

In a verbal triumph, Burton turned his resistance into his own truth. "I don't care if I ever have money," he told me that spring. "I don't like all these people talking about how important money is. I don't care if I live in the middle of a slum, just as long as my house is clean. When I need money, I'll be a bus driver for a while." The next fall he turned up as a Good Humor man, parking his truck in front of the college beneath the elevated railway. Bright as ice cream itself in his uniform, he stood at the curb and greeted his old friends. In the spring, doing business there again, he was ready to explain more. "You have to be yourself," he said. "So many people go to college to be somebody else. These girls with their outrageous notions—to be a doctor or something. Be yourself." While I took this in, I reminded him of his capacity for writing and the capacity to be an individual while in college. The trouble, he said, had been "just college. I worked hard in your course." He said he was reading some books by Richard Wright, whom he had discovered in the first remedial class the previous semester. Though he suggested he might enroll again, he glared at the glass wall of the library, grumbling that he really didn't want any part of it. Identity he had; he was an American decrying materialism and every kind of put-on, an exponent of the individualistic tradition in our culture. The pity was that the culture was so fragmented that the books which might have furthered his views he saw simply as another authority.

A white student in one of the remedial classes also had an authority problem. He had taken a year off before college to go surfing. His first papers were characteristic in their incompetence—run-on sentences, undefined thoughts, chaos. He didn't care. He had given the nineteenth year of his life to surf riding. Bleached from sun or sunlamp, his hair fell over his forehead. Of his family I only knew what he told me —that his parents disapproved of surf riding and surf bumming. Yet he had taken his board on his back and gone to Florida with friends; on the way he had been refused service at one gas station because of his long hair. His parents, objective education, and garage attendants made up the establishment with which he had been doing battle. He said "ain't" more often than "isn't" in spite of, or because of, grammar tests. When I suggested that he said "ain't" in order to attack the older generation, he sputtered denial, but didn't say "ain't" again. After his first unintelligible papers, I began to insist that he write about the sea, his true love— for a surfboard is not a sundeck. The sea was the metaphor on which, in writing, he was able to ride. Thomas Bailey wrote with much grace:

> Here I am bobbing up and down, enclosed in the cockpit of this strange body extension, grasping a double headed paddle, and wondering what to do next.
>
> Ignoring all my fears, I commenced paddling, vigorously slicing the water with wild uneven alternating strokes. I didn't expect any trouble from the waves since they don't discriminate objects riding them, but suddenly fearful thoughts arose, like how does this thing steer, what should I do with the paddle, and how do I get out of the Kayak.
>
> By the time I realized this, the Kayak was traveling backwards down the face of a huge wave with the stern pearling, while the bow swung up and over. I felt as though my lungs would burst, I attempted a last ditch effort to flip back over, and succeeded.
>
> I then spent the next two hours trying to discard the disillusionment of my first ride.
>
> Gaining enough courage to journey out again, I begin planning my ride. I'm in the exploring stages of this sport, but with every stroke of the paddle I felt more confident of mastering this new technique of riding waves. Suddenly I spot a set of outside waves. I begin paddling with all the strength my arms possess. Pulling in a fantastic even rhythm, straining to elude the outside wall. I descend over the first wall, only to be suspended in a valley of water. I turn around to see the wave unleash an unreal amount of power. I see the water being hurled about with such force, and then realize what may happen if I become locked in one of those waves.

Oh, he tumbled an intransitive verb and made other slips here and there. Where there had been no sense of proportion—indeed few clear or complete sentences—now there were sentences with major and secondary parts, balanced in what the textbooks called parallelism. The commas had come in. Verbs were brisk and precise, images were naturally born in "a valley of water." Ideas were right in the language—"body extension," "locked in one of those waves." Thomas will not be able to make his way through college on water, yet he was now nosing his way into the library, reading, he said, Camus. Perhaps he was drawn to Camus by the relentless sun of that writer, by the wide beaches. The personal connection we make with accomplished minds can lead to learning.

In another class, a voice had risen modestly yet clearly from the back of the room when I asked students what they had done during the summer. "I bet I've done something nobody else has. I've been in Phoenix House." The presence of an admitted rehabilitated drug addict surprised me and left the room still. Out of the room full of serious faces, Lyman Daley's shone with calm. In his first paper he made it clear where he stood.

Scag and the South Bronx

I live in the Bronx, one of the five boroughs which make up New York City. But I live in a very special part of the Bronx, the South Side. New York has its ghettoes like Harlem, Brownsville, and Bedford Stuyvesant, but South Bronx is THE ghetto of New York. It has more of everything that nobody else wants, more crime, run-down tenements, welfare recipients, high-school dropouts, venereal disease, unemployment, unwed mothers, but all these ills seem minor compared to the abundance of heroin which travels through the streets of the South Bronx.

It is as easy to get scag as it is to go to the grocery store and buy bread. Dope peddlers standing on street corners, addicts doubled over in blissful stupor, young girls willing to sell themselves for the price of a fix, is what South Bronx is all about. There is a plague spreading over the South Bronx and the plague is dope and it seems destined to strangle the life out of the South Bronx and its people. There is a large sign on a community center building on Simpson Street, and it reads, "LOVE YOUR COMMUNITY." Needless to say this sign is very much out of place in the South Bronx.

Daley later did his term paper on the South Bronx, using research and his own observations. A girl in the class, with dyed red hair and light brown skin, tried to take charge of him. Responding to his revelation on the first day, she had turned around to him—and admonished him from the front row: "I hope you're over that now. You better be over that." Ironically, Cynthia's first paper was on her experiences with cocaine; later in the term she slipped into a funk, but she never stopped trying to reform Lyman Daley. He was doing fine on his own, as she knew from the papers of his we read aloud in the class. Urging him on, she had the proprietary air of a literary godmother, the kind Thomas Wolfe and James Jones have known. "Now you write that term paper," I heard her tell him once. The class was the second remedial course, but Daley was doing so well he could easily have written the term paper and gotten credit for the third course as well. Cynthia stuck unfailingly to his side; he seemed amused and flattered, but retained his detachment, dangling his African beads.

In spite of her classroom passivity, she did turn in a memorable stanza.

Check out your mind
Check out your mind
Check out your black mind

Daley was a fine-featured young man with a slim, wiry build, who invariably wore the suit of the land—dungaree pants and jacket. He condensed a lot of energy and conflict in the light, graceful way he walked, his face often radiating feeling even in repose. Control of feeling showed in his writing. He had an articulate irony bred into his outlook. In a paper called "Summer," he spoke bitterly of the terrible things that had happened that season.

My best friend was sentenced to a long prison sentence for killing an old woman in the summer. And news that a girl I used to go with was now a prostitute, came to my attention in the summer. The two Ortiz brothers who had been my family's next door neighbors for years were killed by police while attempting to rob a liquor store. That was three summers ago. Two summers ago, my brother was found dead, shot full of bullets in the Mekong Delta. We learned later it wasn't bullets he was shot full of. . . .

He was a great admirer of the columnist Pete Hamill, and had learned from reading him. In his rebel form, Daley had a bourgeois vertebra. Both the rebel and the man of standards showed beautifully in a paper prompted by the arrest of H. Rap Brown for allegedly holding up a Manhattan saloon. In it he hit his stride.

RAP

In Roosevelt Hospital, behind a wall of police, in a tight security recovery room, with tubes running into his nose and throat, lies H. Rap Brown. It is ironic that Rap Brown now lies mortally wounded while news of others, until recently inactive revolutionaries, are all around us. News like Huey Newton making a trip to Red China, and Bobby Seale active in the Attica peace talks, and Eldridge Cleaver announcing his return from Algerian exile. Rap Brown had been a fugitive for 17 months and was not heard from. And now the news of his ill-fated saloon holdup descended upon us with the swiftness and force of a wrecking ball. When the Freedom Rides and Martin Luther King's pleas were no longer heeded, Rap Brown was there. When Eldridge Cleaver fled the country and Stokley Carmichael was no longer influential, Rap Brown was there. Rap Brown didn't shoot Medgar Evars and Malcolm X. Rap Brown didn't murder John F. Kennedy. That wasn't Rap Brown blowing Martin Luther King out of America. Rap Brown did not put a bullet into Bobby Kennedy's skull. Rap Brown is not responsible for the Vietnam War. He killed no students at Kent State. He didn't shoot anyone in Watts and Newark. So there is no sense of relief when the police tell us Rap Brown was wounded and arrested, after he and three other men attempted to hold up a Manhattan saloon. There will be some people who will try to say this was a revolutionary act. But there is nothing revolutionary about sticking up a saloon and no one knows this better than Rap Brown. Sticking up saloons does have something to do with being on the run, it does have something to do with being desperate with nowhere to turn. I am not implying excuses for Rap Brown. Men who stick up saloons are potential murderers, they have guns because they are prepared to use guns. And people who think they can use guns on other people should be in jail. Rap Brown is no exception. It was Rap Brown who put everyone on notice when he said, "Violence is as American as cherry pie." Rap Brown was formed by American violence. And until violence has disappeared Rap Brown and men like him will always be around. Rap Brown will go to trial and if found guilty will go away. For Rap Brown the running is over. For Rap Brown the revolution is over.

The student newspaper, *The Black I,* a holdover from the days of student revolution, refused to print this splendid outcry but snidely rebuked those who thought "the revolution was over" in an editorial. A moral code that did not allow for excuses had brought Daley out of his problems. He showed an immunity to the trouble he wrote about. I once asked him if his family were unsettled by the terror he described in the South Bronx, and he said no, that no one worried when his mother walked home from a bus stop late at night coming home from work.

When we read *Native Son* in class he couldn't accept Richard Wright's theme that racism was a subtle poison infecting Bigger Thomas, the black boy who murders twice. While he allowed for the responsibility of society, he thought Wright's son of poverty and prejudice deserved the electric chair. "Give him a life sentence and he would get out and murder someone else. I see people like Bigger Thomas all the time."

At the beginning most of the men in the class took a similar view, while the young women all sought mercy for the criminal-victim. By the end of the discussion, all but Daley would have administered psychiatric help and a life sentence. He stuck with the chair. Thomas, he finally argued, had not only murdered his black girl friend as well as a white girl, but had been insulting and uncaring toward his own mother and sister. With such strong standards, Daley had pulled himself up from what he called "the limbo of heroin addiction."

For a while I felt he was angry with me for my explanation of Bigger as a victim not merely of racism but of fear. His intolerance of Bigger was part of his own strength, but his annoyance at me revealed his sensitivity to the agonizing problems he had overcome. He sailed forth from this class as an accomplished writer. He was one who had faced failure and drawn strength from it. "Drudgery, calamity, exasperation, want," Ralph Waldo Emerson told us long ago, "are instructors in eloquence and wisdom."

4 Getting Over

Two hours long, the class met at eight in the morning two days a week and once in the afternoon. Like many students in the first year of the Open Admissions program at CUNY, James had a long subway ride to York College, which was located in temporary quarters on the ragged edge of Queensborough Community College. The flimsy structures that contained York's classrooms were painted a schoolhouse red, in contrast to Queensborough's new stone and glass buildings.

James came to every scheduled class in our fluorescent-lit, prefab classroom. Normally prompt, he usually took a seat in the front row next to the door. I think that students who sit in the center, front-row are the most serious. I usually worry about those who choose the back corner. Those who sit in the front row on the side seem ambivalent, as though they need the magnetic pull of a teacher.

James was a student in the SEEK program, which brings ghetto students to college with the help of financial aid, counseling, and special remedial programs. A well-proportioned boy in his late teens, with modest features, a modest build, a nice brown face, he had a speaking voice that had the suggestion of song. He had shown absolutely no writing

71

ability in the placement exam, and consequently was assigned to the first of three remedial courses. In my class he struggled against his own insecurities, and his unfamiliarity with writing. His eloquence, which someday might flourish, would emerge only if competence were instilled in him. But the method of teaching language "skills," if the teacher is not careful, may stifle the student's native eloquence.

Whether wearing the thin material of a cheap, but well-pressed suit or the blue jeans of universal youth, James was a collected presence in the class—watching, listening from his corner post. He believed in the miracle of attentiveness. He had thought he could get through by faith and attendance alone. Sitting in the class like someone who regularly attended church—who liked the words and even the sermon—he felt he should be rewarded. When I told him he needed to take the course again, he was stunned.

Early in the first term he made a triumph of error. Having read Richard Wright's short story "The Man Who Lived Underground," the students were to write a tale of their own inspired by Wright's flight and their fancy. I put two sentences on the board, simplifying Wright's opening lines to get them started. "The siren wailed. He was being chased." James hadn't read the story, but he produced an illiterate tale of lilting quality.

> The siren wailed was being chased by men who wont to take his life. but for a year the wailed was not seen. Men from the East and West of the World. came to such for the siren wailed. Many mens die on their ships. Some get sick and went home, but there were men from the north. Who called ther ship the Mad Hunter. for years men such for the wailed one day. some men seen the wailed and went down the way the wailed. The siren wailed knew. he was being chased. the wailed went under the water and he was not seen again.

The king of the deep, nicely named, had swum in his head. The punctuation was added later—bee-bee shots from a trembling hand. "Men from the East and West of the World," the elusive whale, the obsessive hunt—were these from some deep memory of *Moby Dick* or out of the common subconscious of Ishmael? During the next class, he came right up and said, with shame, that he had misread the sentence. Later he told me he had some books about whaling at home, but declined to name any titles. No loss. He had miserably written a story with the elements of good writing in it. Beneath the grammatical chaos lay a rhythm and balance, matching the action. "Men from the East and West of the World came to such for the siren wailed." Without the strain of punctuation or spelling had come assonance, consonance, song. The *d* of *world* echoed in the non-noun *wailed*, a nice off-rhyme; *men* sounded again in *siren,* a non-sentence later; *s*'s and *e*'s wove through the illiteracy, binding the chaos together. Read aloud, the whole paragraph sung like a hymn.

In class his speaking voice often touched on literacy. I'd ask the students if they had heard those past tenses, the *ed*'s at the end of his verbs. They had been there. So had pauses where the periods go. He had spoken in sentences. Students, however illiterate, I had begun to realize, often spoke in complete sentences. I could hear in their speech the form they left out of their writing. I had become more and more convinced that students of writing needed to begin from the way they talked.

Students have been told not to write as they talk so often that writing becomes an awkward act, like walking on stilts. The purpose of this bad counsel is, I suppose, to keep slang out of writing—but students know how to keep it out of their speech and their writing if they want to. If English teachers would only get their students talking about subjects that interest them, they would hear feats of grammar performed in mid-air. In James's spoken sentences there were subordinate and main clauses; he could make natural judgments with his mind. Students, from the ghetto or elsewhere, cannot get away with the slang and grunts of common talk when they write. But when they talk about something important to them, the most illiterate of students approach literacy, and often become correct, even eloquent. They begin to find the tighter voice that good writing demands.

I had been asking students to write their ideas out, but now James made me think that I should work more directly with speech. The next term, especially to get him talking, I brought a tape recorder to class. The tape recorder would not be a crutch, but a record of human sound. The students were to talk about anything that mattered to them; then, playing the tape back, we would hear the beginning of writing. Given a microphone, the students either had to muster their courage or lose their nerve. Most seized it, talked far better than they had written, and sat back in amazement, not only at hearing their own voices, but also at finding that they had voices.

When he got to the microphone, James leaned forward and stared into space and, like anyone formulating an idea, almost visibly reached for it. "This is Negro History Week," he said, stopping where the sentence stopped, but not for long. The voice grew huskier, the words began to flow. "If one people hold down another for a long time, they won't forget it. White people aren't going to give black people what they have a right to have. Black people have got to get things for themselves." The connections were there, the tenses worked, the voice paused at commas, took stock at periods. "Some black people have pictures of Robert Kennedy and Martin Luther King on their walls. But that says blacks haven't done anything by themselves. Blacks have. They have accomplished without whites. Some of the best baseball players in this country have been blacks, some of the best football players too. The people with those pictures on their walls don't know who they are." There, in a spoken paragraph, more than grammar had appeared. Once his premise had been stated, logic prevailed; idea had moved to definition of idea. A force of feeling had created clarity and balance.

When I told him his words would make a fine written paragraph, he was amazed. When he played the tape back, he was pleased at the sound of his oration. Then why couldn't he get the same words on paper? He squinted, and came up with another statement. "The words run and flee. When I try to write, they run away." He couldn't catch them.

Words, I suggested, don't have the power to run on their own. "You're chasing them," I told him. That sobered him.

Like James, many people suffer from a fear of writing. Because writing has always seemed an alien act to them, the words do escape. Because it is taught as a special tongue, it makes some people feel unworthy of it.

In his writing, James showed the marks of dialect—what has come to be called black English: the *ed*, often apparent in his speech, was often missing from verbs that needed past tenses; the third person singular rarely had an *s*.

Black dialect has now become the subject of scholarly study, and while the scholars have tried to create a mighty science—working up mathematical codes for forms that slip off the tongue—they have shown it is merely another pattern of speech formed in a particular culture. Black dialect is not "wrong"; it is simply the way a black child growing up in poverty, North or South, learns to speak—by perfect imitation of those around him.

A speech pattern formed in the South, possibly with African roots, transplanted to the North and varying from place to place, it is above all a variation of standard English, its close cousin. People speaking black dialect will write *he walk* instead of *he walks*. The third person singular omits the *s* everywhere: *he have* instead of *he has; he don't* instead of *he doesn't*. Since the *s* on nouns indicates a plural, there might be a kind of logic in omitting it from singular verbs. But while there is consistency in black dialect as well as in standard English, neither of the grammars can justify itself by logic, since much of any grammar is simply custom.

According to the linguist J. L. Dillard in *Black English*, the dialect goes far beyond the lack of an *s* in the third person singular and the missing *ed* into usages different from the standard. Delving into folk histories of eighteenth- and nineteenth-century slave life and sampling the deep ghetto talk of children primarily in Washington, D.C., today, he finds the past indicated by ample "clues" and the duration of an event indicated by special verb forms peculiar to the dialect. A preference for a singular pronoun over plurals or genders, and the omission of some relative pronouns and of some prepositions—all aspects shocking to grammarians—become, according to Dillard, speech patterns that produce sufficient communication. In showing that a consistent use of forms, however different from the standard, does constitute a grammar and convey clear meaning to its speakers, Dillard takes the arrogance out of white grammatical supremacy. But the sins of specialization lead to a romance with the dialect's origin and an inflation of its use. "Black English" becomes the son of an "ancestral Pidgin English," developed by captured Africans of different tribal languages in order to communicate with each other.

With a full set of complex terminology, Dillard tracks its development from "pidgin" to "creole" to a "basilect"—the extreme dialect of the ghetto today. Fascinated by this extreme, he rejects the influence of rural British dialects used by uneducated white Americans, long held to be the model that blacks learned from. The "Overseer" theory—whereby the East Anglican dialect brought to America and spoken by many nineteenth-century whites took hold in black speech—does not hold up for Dillard. Instead, he offers an indigenous development of dialect by blacks themselves. Though he doesn't find many parallels in black dialect to African languages but sees similarities between Caribbean and black American speech, he overlooks the obvious. Today, accounts of the slave era, such as Alex Haley's *Roots,* suggest a common-sense definition of language development. Anyone today who tries to make himself understood by someone who doesn't speak his language probably simplifies his speech. It is likely that the white man spoke a primitive English to the captured African, and omitted tenses, auxiliaries, pronouns, and prepositions to drive home commands. It was the white man who invented "pidgin," rather than, in some mysterious spontaneity, slaves seeking to bridge the gap between each other. Blacks undoubtedly passed it on from generation to generation and spun it into greater consistency and variation. And variation inevitably occurred, between house slave and field hand, between blacks isolated from educated whites and blacks in daily contact with whites, educated or not.

Dillard allows that all poor blacks do not speak the same dialect. Indeed, he has come up with the fascinating observation—the explanation of which would be even more interesting—that it is chiefly ghetto children under six who speak the pure thing. If teachers and adults in the ghetto community exercise a corrective influence on the child—and more effectively if the child adapts his speech to the more standard patterns he hears—who is it, what force is it, that keeps a dialect pure in the first four or five years of speech? Dillard is offended by the layman's notion that such early speech is "baby talk." But some laymen and even linguists have observed that many adults talk to children in simplified speech. Perhaps the old syndrome—those in command talking down to the helpless—is at work again.

Using the estimate of another scholar although "admittedly incomplete," Dillard says that "approximately 80 percent" of American blacks speak "black English." Since, by his own qualifications, dialect varies from place to place, from person to person, from age to age, one manifestation to another, the statement seems to have no meaning. Influenced by the era of "black pride," Dillard has reached for a cultural unity where no such unity exists. What was perhaps meant as a compliment to racial solidarity has become an insult many blacks resent. Educated blacks view the classification itself as racist. For my students, not yet educated and showing random peculiarities of grammar, the classification is irrelevant.

No one can measure the extent and influence of the dialect. Often the dialect pattern begins with forms that are only a letter away from the standard. "Code switching," one of the livelier linguistic terms, occurs when a speaker consciously changes a speech pattern from dialect to standard. Some younger blacks switch back and forth to suit the occasion, whereas educated blacks usually speak a consistent standard grammar. The older they are, the more ghetto children live in two cultures. The samples of speech by ghetto children show the use of both standard and dialect forms, often a confused mixture of the two. This seems inevitable. For although home and the ghetto street are surely strong teachers, the world outside the ghetto also influences language. My students read the *Daily News,* the *Amsterdam News, Ebony,* or other magazines; they watch television and listen to radio, they go to the movies. They do encounter standard English.

Dillard has suggested that black dialect be used to teach children to read and to write. This might work in classroom situations, rural or urban—if the dialect form were drawn from the children themselves in order to show them the equivalent form in standard American. But the texts written in black dialect would create a great deal of confusion for some of the following reasons: There is no common dialect to establish; not only do usages vary, but—since dialect is only a spoken language—whatever forms were decided on would have no standard spelling. Dillard and company ask for instant language creation, but such a thing is impossible. As Elizabethans battled with Old English, as classicists contended with Elizabethans, as Americans came to disagree with British English, Dillard and other linguists will argue among themselves.

At an experimental South Carolina school, Gullah, the deep dialect of the Carolina coast and islands is honored as a respectable language and used as an aid in teaching standard English. It is taught as a second language. Wholly an oral tradition—it developed first because of the isolation of the island plantations, and was preserved until now by geographic isolation from integrated communities—written Gullah is not used much, except in student poetry. Using the dialect surely honors those who base their identity on it; and when an oral tradition is so deep-rooted, writing it down and using it in teaching "legitimizes" it. Many people who speak only dialect are ashamed of their speech. Giving dialect written form restores to its users self-respect.

Getting an oral language codified requires a Homer or a

Shakespeare, with large tales to tell, not a group of linguists sorting out prepositions. The oral supremacy of Gullah has a fair chance of lasting in the Carolinas, though even the oral patterns change under the influence of standard forms and, now, of television. Whatever status teachers and linguists give to dialect, the dialect—even where deep-rooted like Gullah—is still subject to change and attrition. In a few papers from urban blacks, I've found two place indicators in one clause: "the old town in Georgia where my grandmother lives at." But the extra preposition is unaccompanied by any other shadows of Gullah.

If linguists should try to create a written black dialect—beyond the needs of a particular area—they will either have to use the most extreme denominator—Gullah—or end up with a variation of standard American. Language, as history shows us, gets codified only by custom, and is sanctioned by the authority of the printing press. With the exception of a few experimental poems, even black writers haven't ventured into the century-long business of language creation.

Ethnic and race oriented, the linguists not only ignore the child's exposure to both dialect and standard forms, but also assume that his pride is at stake. He must be given the choice of using dialect if he wants. Dillard's proposal that college students be allowed to write term papers in "Negro Nonstandard" is funny. The dialect user might well pronounce the *g* at the end of *writing,* but he would misspell his own language and write *writin.* Even if he were writing the paper on a black author—a good idea—he would find that writer using standard American grammar. The "black English" belief is really a "separate but equal" doctrine rising out of the militance of the 1960s, reflecting all the sentimentality about the spontaneous development of "pidgin" and "basilect." The linguists have made people aware that black dialect is not "wrong," but that it is picked up like any other spoken grammar; and they're right in knowing that the standard grammar will have to be "internalized" before it is used automatically.

Ghetto students need the chance to emulate good writing.

Rather than offering a "choice" of two dialects in courses that would honor both as equal, schools can teach standard American grammatical forms, where necessary, by translation. When my students exhibit the missing *s* syndrome in their work, I write equations on the blackboard between the "spoken" and "written" form; when I hear some pleasing "down-home" verb—"my mother talk to us about studying" —I point out the difference and ask the student to conjugate the spoken and compare it with the written verb form. Inevitably there's a bit of play acting in "code switching"; but it may be the first step to "internalizing" a grammar as the student corrects his own work.

Confusion between the standard and dialect form, found by Dillard in ghetto children, is abundant at the college age. Obviously, some internalizing has already begun. An *ed* will take hold in one sentence, disappear where it is needed in the next, and sometimes fall down with a thud—he *hurted.* The *s* on the third-person singular will come and go. There's no personality loss in the application of an *s* or an *ed* or in spelling, as long as the student's capacity for thought and feeling is respected.

Scientists that they would be, the "sociolinguists" give microscopic attention to the structure of language while missing its real achievements. Metaphor, idiom, and sound pattern elude them not just aesthetically, but as sources for teaching. The inventions of black American idiom—one of its genuine contributions to the standard American language —Dillard dismisses as the work of a black elite. But eloquence rises from the needs of a people, from their common experience. Those who may have coined a phrase find it taken back and refined by its users.

The black church has been a rich source of language. The language of the church is grammatically close to, or a perfection of, standard American, and elevates our common tongue. When we hear a black sermon, we hear the voice raised to an eloquence not found in much public discourse today. One may notice an *s* missing here or there in some black sermons, but the language is biblical, American, Elizabethan. The church and gospel-music language is as much a teacher as the street—and a better one. "Code switching" is made easier by the church's influence. Recently I heard a hymn in a black church, and I couldn't tell whether I heard "pidgin" or forced rhyme: "One day when I was loss / They nailed him on the cross / And it was the blood of me." But I did discover in a socially approved form an "error" I find in the writing of young blacks. I've found whites, too, confusing *loss* and *lost.*

In James Russell Lowell's once celebrated *Bigelow Papers,* a collection of fictionalized letters from a New England farmer, and in Eugene O'Neill's *Desire under the Elms,* forms now called black dialect leap from the page. Some black speech forms have so much in common with rural American dialect of a century ago that they are unrepentant siblings to the way many white Americans talked, especially in New England and the South. In denying this relationship linguists lose the large view of history for the small. They make much of the black use of *be* with a pronoun and claim it suggests the continuing, or "durative," nature of something: *he be working* means that the man has a steady job. But in *Desire under the Elms,* faithfully reproducing mid-nineteenth-century rural New England dialect, a Yankee farmer says to his sons, "This be my house," fixing his permanent ownership as well as a link with "black dialect." The American *ain't,* used in preference to *isn't* or *am not,* comes from the mouths of the *nouveau riche* and gentry in the novels of Henry James and William Dean Howells, not just in the dialogue of Twain's country bumpkins. The same characters speaking in James and Howells emit strange verb forms, leaving off *s*'s where we put them today: "His wife don't keep any girl, your mother wan't ashamed," proclaims Howell's Silas Lapham, a paint manufacturer in Boston, 1875, risen from a Vermont farm. In prayers still said in white churches, the past tense of *build* is not *built* but *builded,* as a black student oblivious of irregular verbs might write today. The descendants of early rural American white speech are black dialect and the white speech of Appalachia;

the two are not identical but enough alike to suggest a common ancestor. And the ancestor of American dialects, black and white, is, of course, rural England.

The presence of nonstandard forms throughout America makes a more important point than one of historical legacy. "Standard English," until sometime in this century, has had a tenuous hold on American speech and, indeed, in the history of English-speaking people, is a modern form, coming into style among a Cambridge-Oxford-London elite in the seventeenth and eighteenth centuries. In England, sanctioned by books and print, it became the upper-class language. Country gentry coming to London became, in effect, bilingual, speaking "proper" English for social reasons in the city, reverting to the dialect in the fields back home. To this day, "be" is an all-purpose verb in English rural dialects, as it is in black dialect. Lower-class English people, rural or urban, revel in double negatives, and in cases where an adverb would be correct stubbornly use an adjective.

A dialect, in spite of the honor heaped on its structure by linguists, is simpler in structure than the more sophisticated language. The latter, for instance, offers a range of precision in its various past tenses; it honors sound in its use of the article *an* before a vowel. The rural English dialect, coming to the new world with rural English immigrants, became, with regional modifications, the spoken language of nineteenth-century America. Dillard, in denying its influence on black speech, offers the Germanic or North European origin of many overseers in the South as evidence. But wherever overseers or other whites came from originally, they too learned the language of rural America, a white dialect born in England, nurtured in American villages, on farms and prairies. Just as it was passed on to non-English-speaking immigrants, so it was passed on to blacks. The simpler nonstandard English fit America's needs.

Our schools, striving mightily for a higher life than the plow or the machine, have striven to wipe out the nonstandard as "wrong." When the rich cadence and pleasing sound of black speech—or its literary cousin in O'Neill's *Desire*

Under the Elms—is heard today, it is apparent that dialect can be a powerful speech, learned by ear—a song sung perfectly by people who may not be able to read the notes. While it is important for historical, among other, reasons for a country to maintain pockets of dialect, the need for teaching standard American English in our schools is clear. It does have more sophisticated possibilities of expression; it is the only language with a literature.

Unlike France, Italy, and Spain, where regional dialects, persisting for centuries, have produced a literature, American dialects haven't. Dialect appears in the dialogue of American novels and plays, thanks to the ear of astute writers, but we are too much of a melting pot to have an official bilingualism, as European countries in effect do. People do speak and write Parisian French—or Castillian Spanish—while fiercely holding on to their regional dialects of Provençal or Basque. Here, "incorrect" speech patterns mix with correct. Those distinctive forms that persist in speech—New England working people of diverse ethnic backgrounds still say "boughten" instead of "bought"—are bumps of the past that refuse to be levelled. If we are lucky, regional idiom—as well as accent—transcending different grammars, will survive, partly because local TV announcers, as well as parents, don't easily give up an inheritance. Language is richer for regionalism.

American schools aren't in the business of changing speech but of establishing a national written language. Only grammar needs to be standardized. The myth of equality, of being one nation, drives us necessarily toward a common grammar. But regional or individual idiom, as long as such idioms serve sense, have a place in writing. Since writing must rise from speech, the idiom of the country must be permissible. However, the myth of equality, which celebrates the worth of every person—although not every person speaks with grammatical perfection—makes it difficult to "teach" a common grammar. People want to pull the grammar down to their level. As English teachers struggle, as they have for two centuries now, to maintain correct usage, they face egalitarian impulses and conditions. To say that a person's grammar is "wrong," when it may have been learned from a culture or just harem-scarem, is to tell him that his identity is wrong, that he is inferior; it makes "education" more difficult for him. This is still being done to blacks today, just as it was done long ago at psychic cost to whites, native and immigrant.

The attempt to declare one grammar "correct," all others "wrong," has furthered the rebellion against correctness. The solution in education is not to usher a theoretical dialect into the classroom, to let students write it, and thus throw their language into further confusion. The solution is to respect the identity of individuals and the existence of different grammatical forms—and to educate the individual in the standard grammar, which really isn't new to him anyway. The battle for a standard American grammar can be won as much by the attitude in teaching as by what is taught.

If we were a class society, where people's stations were fixed, the writing problem would be simpler. Those who were born into high language would write it; those who wanted to rise would gladly learn it. A woman from Barbados, who wrote smooth standard English, let me know that there was no tolerance of dialect in her British school. She always knew the dialect was "wrong." In the British or French educational systems of the Caribbean, a few blacks are selected for limited places in the academically superior schools; the rest are left to live in their dialect. The chosen students may suffer the scars of leaving behind their "first" language and all that it may represent, but I doubt it—at least it hasn't seemed that way to me in my encounters with British- and French-educated blacks. But random selection in the face of need is not the American way. We are too democratic for that— though it might be wiser if we didn't make everybody think he should or could go to college. America has always tried "to educate everybody," one way or another. Education, in spite of its failures, is still seen as the way of civilizing all the natives.

Dialect, I tell my students, is a common American situation. The children of immigrants—Jews, Italians, Poles, Irish —have had to break away from a dialect or language of their parents. To use the standard grammatical form need not be a betrayal, but a seizing of a right of citizenship. The black writers we read, none of whom are traitors to race, write in standard American.

If a student wants to bring his creative powers into the larger world, then he'll need the standard grammar. But the style of his speech and his natural vocabulary can bring distinction to his writing. Here is where the balance lies between the self and the world. Let the world have its grammar and the self evolve its own style, from its own culture. In fact, black speech has had, and still has, a large influence on American language. Even some academics admit what many Americans know: blacks have made a powerful, often inspiring, use of American language. Not only Martin Luther King, but the jive artist, who may be lost to the church, has influenced his country. Tell the students the truth. There's history to keep as well as to leave behind.

In *The American Language,* H. L. Mencken marks the Jacksonian era, when frontiersmen not only came into the White House but also into their own, as the time when "the voice of America took on its characteristic tone colors, and the speech of America began to differentiate itself unmistakably from the speech of England. . . . On the levels below the Olympians, a wild and lawless development of the language went on, and many of the uncouth words and phrases it brought to birth gradually forced themselves into more or less good usage." Americans began to respect their native talent. Webster brought out his distinctive American dictionary and American writers began listening to their native tongue.

Language is perhaps the main melting pot we have. For, while the educated and even the Anglophiles kept a sensible lid on new expression, the uneducated folk offered up a bubbling creativity that, where useful and bold, took hold on all levels of society. Beginning with a release of national invention in the Jeffersonian era, the first half of the nineteenth century gave us such now-conventional verbs as *affili-ate, collide, jeopardize, placate,* and *bluff* (made from nouns), and such blazing images as *run into the ground, take a back seat, keep one's eyes peeled, raise Cain, played out, under the weather, on the fence,* and *true blue.* Much of the national language has always come from the uneducated in America —as it did in Elizabethan England—although newspapers, movies, and now television are becoming innovators themselves. Today the folk genius comes quite obviously from the black poor, meeting their necessities with the same vigor as backwoodsmen did over a century ago. It was the black poor who, coining the phrase, were first "ripped off."

Social science and verbal imitations of technology today lead to cumbersome prose. In contrast, blacks have created language out of need, for human use. "Bread" is one of their inventions. When I was a boy my father, a son of Yankees, used "dough" for money, and I still do. Whites and blacks, at different times, reached for the same yeast, but blacks keep appealing to the senses. Now that people buy their loaves baked and packaged, "bread" may supplant "dough," no matter how much I happen to prefer the original. White immigrant groups have improved our cooking and given us food names, but have had only a slight effect on the language because, however forceful the terms, they are foreign. (I tell a black class about the Yiddish term *chutzpah,* for colossal nerve; they like it; *you have to have chutzpah to write.*) The Yiddish ending *nik* has been applied to American words— beatnik—and generally enriched the language. Many black terms are ironic uses of standard words, and have been in use for a generation or more. Much of the early influence came from jazz, which first brought black experience to whites. For instance, the words "kick" (as in *I get a kick out of you*) and "send" (as in *that really sends me*) received new meaning. The greater influence of black slang is coincident with the civil rights movement and the Vietnam war. The more whites became aware of blacks, the more they heard. And the more the young became disillusioned with America, the more black ironies spoke for them.

Clarence Major, a young black writer, has made a much-needed dent in the mystery of black slang in his *Dictionary of Afro-American Slang*. Beneath black vernacular he sees "a whole sense of violent unhappiness," and finds it "a medium of self-defense against a world demanding participation and at the same time laying a booby-trap network of rejection and exploitation . . . in essence, it is a natural attempt to counteract the classic and dreary weight of political and social oppression, and at a very basic level of human experience." White middle-class kids use—as if they invented them—the common ironies of black kids: "bad" meaning good, "crazy" meaning fine, "mean" meaning wonderful.

I suspect that black speech has a spiritual content to which Americans instinctively respond. Like black music, black language is a testament of human spirit asserting itself in the face of suffering. Black history in America is a highly charged metaphor of everybody else's experience. The extermination of Jews in Germany is probably the only experience that surpasses the oppression of blacks in America. Americans are touchy about prejudice because prejudice has touched their pasts. Not only do we think of ourselves as a nation settled by the oppressed, but Americans are still uprooted by industrialism and mobility and have felt the crush of senseless war, the indifference of institutions. Black language offers metaphors of resistance and joy that some Americans take to gladly—some to be fashionable, but all without shame. The term *make it,* originally black slang, is now part of the American vocabulary without credit to its originators, as are numerous other idioms—*turn on, get high, drop out, with it.*

Slang works its way into the written language only when it invents a term for something that has not existed before, or describes a set of circumstances more vividly than conventional language. Black slang is the language for modern discoveries; it will last as long as the discovery itself. The term *hang-up* has won a place because the psychological stasis it describes simply wasn't widespread before; it is surely more descriptive than its pale synonyms, problem or neurosis. The

same for *uptight,* giving the physical sensation of something
we had thought of only as tension. Some black slang, such
as *bag,* happens to repel me. Yet I can imagine a sentence
where *bag,* in proper juxtaposition, would carry the right
sting. *Getting out of Vietnam was not President Nixon's bag.*
"The history of English, like the history of American and
every other living tongue," Mencken reminds us, "is a history of vulgarisms that, by their accurate meeting of real
needs, have forced their way into sound usage, and even into
the lifeless catalogue of grammarians." Surely not all of black
speech, rising from distress and poverty, will make its way
into the regular language, just as much of the frontier coin-
age a century ago bubbled up and then disappeared.

Black speech has invented not only words, but idioms. In
the idiom rests originality and power, contributing energy
amid more formal terms. The modern movement in poetry
and prose is modern because, among other things, it honors
the vernacular, drops it into elegant cadences.

James, when his writing began to improve after the session
with the tape recorder, showed how black idioms can con-
tribute vitality. Though some students had tape recorders of
their own and others used the ones in the college language
lab, he was too broke to buy one and too distracted to use
the college facility. But he was making headway. Splattered
through his notebook were unfinished compositions with
marvelous phrases, which I spotted when I went over his
work. He often wrote about James Brown, the soul singer,
a hero of his. About halfway through the term he turned in
a complete paper about his idol.

James Brown has really paid his dues. He was a product of
poverty. As a youth Mr. Brown saw many Days of hunger
and tears. But through all of his suffering he kept the faith.
First faith in himself, secondly the loving faith of his race.
Even during those bleak days James was positive he would
one Day make it and make it big. He made mistakes just like
everyone else in the world. But he chose not to linger in
sorrow but to move on to success. Today Mr. Brown has

made his dream into reality. He is the number one of Soul music or Rhythm and Blues as some people choose to label his style of singing. Mr. Brown has not forgotten his background and most of all his people, the Black people. He has devoted much of his time, energy, and finance to show the black people his Deep sincerity and understanding. More power to Mr. Brown.

"To pay one's dues" is a bit of black vernacular no one should have difficulty in understanding. According to *The Dictionary of Afro-American Slang*, it means "to suffer as a result of race prejudice; to have come up the hard way." It brightened its dour successor, "product of poverty." Best of all, it came from the "ear," free to use its sense of sound. The *a* in "James" paved the way for the *a* in "paid." If Brown's first name had been Richard, it wouldn't have worked as well; indeed the writer, sensitive to sound, working from sound, might not have used it. The passage had proper sentences in it and, in spots, was nicely balanced. For research, I think James may have used a record-jacket blurb; some of the phrases had the scent of a blurb. Yet there was sincerity in his capitalizing almost every D. When, just to let him know I couldn't be taken in, I asked how come after a series of messy papers he was so clear on James Brown, he said gravely that James Brown was a great man.

In James's character many ribbons seemed to be woven. He often seemed to me to be several delightful fellows all in one. A devout churchgoer, he was director of his church's choir and offered that as an excuse for not getting his work done. Still, he thought Martin Luther King was too cautious. Malcolm X was his hero. Proud of race, sensitive to white prejudice, James didn't hold back from whites in strain or resentment. At least with me he was a charmer. He would compliment me in the middle of class on the suit I was wearing.

The first day of the second term (he was repeating the course), he asked with what I could only think was a false interest, "Are we going to read Du Bois?" since he had gotten little from reading the great black father the term before. When his interest went sour over a grammatical problem I was pointing out, he looked up with a faint smile and said, "That's the way I talk at home." I hadn't offered home remedies as a cure for illiteracy.

Not long into the second term he was able to write short compositions on assigned subjects and write them perfectly. He wrote one of them in class on the nineteenth-century whaling industry. *Moby Dick* must have been in his library or memory. I began to wonder and asked him if he had a photographic memory. He didn't answer. One week later, when he came up with the right answer in class, he grinned and told me, "I have a photographic memory."

James lived at home with his mother, a "domestic," his counselor told me. He had failed all his courses the first term, all of them remedial: English, speech, and math. He had real poverty problems hounding him. While he was collecting the stipend for an unmarried student—thirty-five dollars every two weeks—he was spending a lot of time, energy and frustration trying to qualify for the fifty-five-dollar award, which went to students with wives or children to support. "But I'm the man of the house," he told me, his hands thrust into his pockets. "I got to work to bring home the bread." His mood showed in his walk. Ordinarily, it was brisk and bouncy. After he failed all his first-term courses, he seemed very sluggish. Looking down at his shoes, he told me he might join the air force. If he flunked out, he'd be drafted anyway. In the air force he'd get money to send home.

Our conversations usually took place after class, as we walked across the campus. To advise someone who is poor when you are not, to understand without condescension, is hard—and I managed it in broken sentences, my way out of embarrassment. I was aware that he would have to make a choice between college and getting a job. I advised him to forget the extra stipend if he couldn't get it, to develop discipline in studying. The half hour or so he told me he spent on a paper was not enough. But, he said, he had to have a job to earn money.

"What do you work at?"

"Oh, a couple of us paint houses when people want us."

"How often?"

"Most every afternoon and Saturdays."

With the term to finish, I told him he should put the money worries aside and deal with them in the summer. I asked him how much time he spent with the choir—his pride —as organizer, director, arranger. He didn't answer. If he really wanted to go to college, I told him, he had to make college his first choice.

The conversation was repeated several times, and each time he left with resolution. He was going to spend time that night doing the papers he owed. But fewer and fewer papers came in; and then, for the first time, he began missing class. A couple of times he told me a cousin had died, a common excuse among my students. Many cousins were dying that term.

In his written classwork James still had to be urged to put on verb endings and commas. I accomplished this by asking him to read his sentence aloud. Lo and behold, the *ed* or the *s* was right there on his tongue. I'd ask if the right ending had gotten stuck somewhere in his elbow, for it had started out in his voice. The structure of sentences has its shadow in the human form. I hadn't been aware of this until the term before when another student, who was turning his verbs into participles, drove me to the discovery. Desperately trying to make a distinction that so far remained unclear to my students, I leaped to connections. "You've cut the heart out of that sentence. Put an *ing* on the verb and the sentence collapses." A little later, I accused him of trying open-heart surgery.

That closely connected, alive and energetic system, the human body, is an apt metaphor for the structure of language. Language itself must be alive. Out of my expeditions in the classroom, I developed an analogy into an exercise. Given to students to punctuate, it is an explanation of how sentences occur and why punctuation comes in. It seems to help. I've found that, with most students, commas and periods begin to appear regularly and rightly, without more urging, after using it.

 a sentence is a separate statement it is like a little country its boundaries are a capital letter at the beginning and a period at the end within its territory it may have districts such as introductory or subordinate clauses when these districts push against the rest of the sentence they are marked off from the rest of the sentence by a comma
 a sentence is also like the human body the verb is its heart without a heart a sentence collapses into a fragment its subject is its head and gives the sentence direction the secondary elements of a sentence are the arms of the main part these may begin with *when* or *if when* or *if* clauses depend on the main part and cannot be amputated from it by a period
 some sentences have equal parts joined together by *and* or *but* equal parts join hands but an unequal part hooks on like a finger to a hand if either an unequal or equal part is heavy enough it is marked off from the rest of the sentence by a comma like the human body sentences fit together in closely related parts

When students read this aloud, they come to natural pauses—short and long—and if they can't find where the commas and periods belong in the first reading, they read it again and do. I have found grammar books useful as dictionaries of error to which a student may refer, but grammar books ignore the tactile and sensory aspect of writing. I have read current advice on writing that ignores grammar in the name of developing the senses, creativity. But grammar is not separate from the senses, but a form through which the senses find clarity. Writing becomes anthropomorphic—because it is an expression of man. It has mysterious human connections. Verbs are the heart because they supply a sentence with energy and allow it to move. A good sentence is balanced, as the body is balanced, with equal weight on either side. The whole weight does not go into a main clause, but into its limbs, allowing the sentence to stretch. Style is like the grace of an athlete or dancer. As the dancer rises, so a sentence ascends toward its importance. It does not come down at the end with a thud, but climbs—as feeling climbs —to a peak. The end of one sentence is a springboard to another. Paragraphs fit together into closely related parts. Style does not come from learning inductive and deductive methods of reasoning. Methods may instill paralysis.

A paper should begin where it begins. The strongest hunch a student has in his head about a subject is the best start, for thought breeds thought. Rather than a stilted introduction or summary, the first sentence should be an open door to an interesting room. Then the mind should be able to move around, to windows, doors, stairs. Rather than framing topic sentences every five lines, the student should think specifically and let the specific lead to something whenever it can. A paper should always advance to the end, not to a summary. Let it end with a nugget that illustrates, or in a knot that ties separate strands together. Let writing grow from itself. Topic sentences? Introductions? Why don't English teachers look at writers? They won't find neat formulas there.

James and his contemporaries not only have to practice writing but also need to practice grammar. They need to think about language. If they only regurgitate what they hear on television, if they never read, they will never become comfortable with writing. James's confusions were frequent, and representative of confusions I have encountered in both black and white students: *mine* for *mind, past* for *passed, worst* for *worse, were* for *where,* as well as an unending confusion of *there* and *their, its* and *it's, your* and *you're.* A white student with an admirable imagination and a terrible lack of practice really sent me with *why'll* for *while.* Yet, back in the mind somewhere, because the words have been encountered in print, a glimmer of the right usage exists. Over and over again, I would ask what a misspelled or incomprehensible word was, and I would hear them say it correctly, even spell it correctly. The writer's hand is so unsure the mind does not control it: a student meaning *wont* writes *when.*

Lists of irregular verbs help, if the ear is also brought into play. Did you ever hear the word *"hurted"?* Students can understand grammar by analogy, but not by rote. Irregular verbs are highly individualistic; they indeed "do their own thing." When sentences are wordy, teachers should write the sick sentence on the board and ask the students what the most important part is, underline it, then subordinate or tighten the rest. Some words do subdue insolent parts of a sentence: *as* and *while, if* and *when.* Teachers can sharpen not only their students' sense of connections in writing but also their ability to say what they mean. An active verb in an active voice carries the weight of the idea. It is possible to show how language works, how ideas grow from detail, how detail is used to build a point, in Op Ed columns from *The New York Times* as well as in essays and novels. And if students don't know the meaning of the word *invoke,* they should be asked to figure it out from the words surrounding it; then add, with further examples of its use, the precise definition.

Basic College English (New Century), a fine workbook published in response to the need for remedial work in college, covers a range of basic problems in pamphlets devoted to verb agreement, pronouns, misused words, spelling. It explains the principle and puts the student to work on examples or usage. The pamphlets, provided with Magic Markers, have some of the fun of a hunt and are self-teaching. The marker is an eraser that, if rubbed on the right line, shows the student he has made the right choice. Many workbooks offer stilted sentences and starchy passages for study, but Louise Roberts' *Teach Yourself How to Write* (Harper & Row), taking passages from vigorous Americans beginning with Ben Franklin, offers lively examples and interesting passages to correct. Workbooks can be helpful as a supplement to exoneration, blackboard examples, and copies of student writing for class correction; in this era of larger classes, they can be used by the weak writer on his own as well as in class. Where workbooks and dictionaries, where priming the student's ear and prodding his writing, aren't enough, he should be sent to a writing clinic or skills center where, with a tutor, he can conjugate verbs and go over first drafts. "Practice, practice, practice," said the elderly Jewish lady to the tourist in New York who asked, "How do you get to Carnegie Hall?" But tutorial help alienates some students; and budget cuts have put such tutorial programs in jeopardy.

With few of the workbooks done and with less than a month to go before the end of the term, James had completed only one composition. I had given him a lot of papers to rewrite, but they stayed in his maze of a notebook, unchanged. His punctuation was improving, but his latest work was far less eloquent than his piece on James Brown. He demonstrated surprising ignorance. In response to Richard Wright's essay "The Ethics of Living Jim Crow," he wrote as if Jim Crow were the author, narrating his experience. History was lost to him.

No single approach works in getting the best out of students. Anger I've hardly used at all. But with three weeks to go, James's promises unkept, I did get mad. The other students were writing a response to Langston Hughes' *Tales of Simple.* James came to class late and admitted he hadn't read the assignment. I told him that he would never learn to write if he didn't do the work. I asked him to leave the class and go somewhere and read the assignment; I would find him a place. Wounded, James looked like a man thrown out of his own home. He still lived with the illusion that getting to class would bring him grace. If I couldn't grapple with his poverty, I could deal with his illusions. I took him to my office and showed him a desk. Twenty minutes later I went back and got him. I asked what he thought of what he had read. He said it made him think of how awful life in Harlem was. Write about that, I urged. The next day he brought this in.

Thinking of Harlem makes me feel everything and everybody is doing bad. It makes me think of hard times. A life full of unhappiness, brothers and sisters trying to do their thing to make a living. Kids up and down the streets having not anything to do. Many people out of jobs. Large numbers of familys living in old houses with rats and all kinds of bugs. People with a family of 6, or 7 living in three rooms. People taking off other people just to get some money to get some pot. The world is pushing human beings with things that we are just not able to take. life, some people say, is what you make it, but I know better. There are things that come into our life sometimes that make us turn the way of our life all around.

There are teachers, unaware of our language, who would dismiss the paragraph because the middle contains sentence fragments. But phrases can and do stand alone when short and emphatic and, as here, in a logical sequence. He had started writing sentences again when there were statements to make. In the last line, he had written a sentence worthy of the sensibility I had heard in his voice but only glimpsed in his writing. Where other students might have stopped, he had gone on to a tragic perception. He had thought.

Before taking the final exam, James wrote a major paper, a response to a chapter from *The Autobiography of Malcolm X*. We had discussed the chapter in class, and his essay showed he had listened; some of his observations paralleled some I had made. But the piece was his own. While it still demonstrated an awful unfamiliarity with language, it was well put together. It had style and resonance. Vernacular, falling amid conventional terms, lightened the load, sharpened the point.

From reading the excerpts of Malcolm X autobiography I can identify with him and his black struggle. The name of his game was to get over. When we as blacks pursue the struggle that is relevant to the Black cause we must get over. no matter how we get over, the purpose is to get over. From childhood Brother malcolm encountered racial hatred and prejudices. His hatred can be traced back to the death of his father who were murdered by white man. Then his hate can also be traced back to when the Welfare checks became a pass for the white man to enter into the lives and try to control their minds. Once they saw that his mother had weakened they took defenot steps to take him away and at this point succeeded in separating the family. He had to learn earlier in life that survival is a main factor and no matter how you accomplish your goal just be sure to win, cheating included. He learned early that in order to get over you had to out smart or be as smart as the next man. An early lesson that he learned in life was—"anytime you find someone more successful than you are, especially when you're in the same business, you know they're doing something that you aren't." After his mother suffered a complete break down and the court order was to take them away, he viewed this as legal modern slavery —however unintentional. Even though the family was split up they remained close in mind. This is the thing that we as black Brothers and Sisters should do today. Even though there may be conflicts in our way of survival we must stick together if it's only in mind. One way or the other we must get over.

The paper was held together by style. Perhaps there was the structure of the hymn in it, from a choirmaster. His voice was there. That fine piece of vernacular—"to get over," known to blacks but new to me—came on stronger and stronger, picking up the momentum of all that went before, until it became a refrain. He had used natural words in a natural order, stumbling at times. He had thought out a specific into the general.

When I told him that I liked the paper, he was pleased, but I don't think he was surprised. In spite of all his trouble he always had confidence in himself. His faith—at first unwarranted and blind—had led him forward. But now he thought his obligations were finished. Outside, he looked around at the muddy campus and asked if he really had to take the exam. He told me he wanted to go to Baltimore, and that he had already arranged a ride. I told him he had obligations here. The exam had to be taken. He had to choose his priorities. He looked as if I had robbed him of a summer job, but he took the exam anyway. The course was a pass-fail, and I passed him. I hoped he would continue to garner further strength in the next two remedial courses.

After the last class, we walked across the hillside, now drying out in the spring sun.

"You've really given me confidence in myself as a black person," he said.

Stunned by the compliment, I instinctively felt for a restrained response. "As a person," I said, "and as a black person."

"You showed me things in myself I could use. I didn't know they were there before."

Writing is our brotherhood. I wanted him to go on—and to grasp reality. "You're a person in your writing, but not a well-disciplined person in your work yet. You can learn to be a well-disciplined person."

We shook hands, turned, and walked our different ways. I hope what he found stays him well, for English was the only course he passed. The other two, speech and math, he failed for the second time, and he was dismissed from the program. Too much time in too many years had been lost. There wasn't time enough. Too many real distractions had made sure of that.

5 Open Admissions

When in the fall of 1970 the City University of New York launched an Open Admissions program, it was responding to militant political pressure and demonstrating the tradition of American higher education to serve democratic need. Brought on by a successful campus revolution in which militant students had occupied buildings and closed down classes, the new policy guaranteed college admission, regardless of grades, to anyone with a New York City high school diploma. A renowned public university proud of its high academic standards and with its own history of educating the white immigrant poor, CUNY not only advanced the open admissions policies of contemporary community colleges to four-year institutions, but repeated the helter-skelter democracy of public higher education in the nineteenth century.

Most of the students who appear in this book would not have been in four-year colleges without Open Admissions or SEEK, its ally in extending educational opportunity; some would not have been at CUNY without its long-held policy of free tuition, abruptly ended in 1976 when Open Admissions itself was curtailed. However admission practices might tighten or relax, however much New York City's budget crisis might shrink and limit the huge public univer-

sity, the new students brought to CUNY by Open Admissions are representative of problems and promise, old and
reborn, in American public colleges.

Public-supported colleges now have been forced, out of
need and conviction, to assume once more the principles of
the Morrill Act of 1862, which set out "to promote the
liberal and practical education of the industrial classes in the
normal pursuits and professions in life." In place of the social
conscience of the land-grant act, which, drawn up by a Vermont senator and signed into law by President Lincoln,
launched the state university system, the 1970s substituted
Open Admissions. The original act brought barely educated
rustics to newly constructed colleges, and the later policy
brought poorly educated blacks and whites to confused
urban campuses. Since few high schools existed west of the
Alleghenies, the start of state universities was as educationally hazardous as the start of Open Admissions, supported
by the feeblest of high school preparation. Just as CUNY
today offers remedial work to college students with an
"eighth grade reading level," so in their early years our now
prestigious state universities were giving ninth to twelfth
grade work to rural youth who had barely gone beyond the
three R's.

The American white majority made an aggressive state
university system out of meager beginnings. One of the great
achievements of the land-grant colleges was to stimulate the
development of a high school system.* Ironically, CUNY's
Open Admissions policy has shown the New York City public high school system to be scandalously indifferent to education.

But New York college and secondary school students are
not alone in their troubles. Everywhere, the pitiful preparation of college-bound students joins with many other pressures to put the American high school under fire.

Written into our very ethos, still sputtering forth today, is

*For much of my information on state universities, I am indebted to Allan Nevins's
excellent history, *The State Universities and Democracy,* University of Illinois Press,
1962.

the idea enunciated in the Ordinance of 1787 which set aside land for "seminaries of higher learning": "religion, morality, and knowledge being necessary to good government and the happiness of mankind, schools and the means of education shall be forever encouraged." The origin of CUNY in 1847 shows how deep the democratic impulse in American higher education lies. "Open the doors to all," declared Townsend Harris at the dedication of the city's new Free Academy, a forerunner of City College and the start of the City University. "Let the children of the rich and poor take their seats together and know of no distinction save that of industry, good conduct, and intellect." "Intellect" was more likely to be found in the urban East, which started a secondary school system long before the rest of the country. Yet in the early 1900s, City College, still the single unit of what was to become a university of many colleges, was inundated by ill-prepared students, unable to read or write English well enough for college work, who were given what was in effect remedial classes. Jefferson's idea was that an "aristocracy ... of talents" would emerge without regard to "wealth and birth" from successive stages of education ending at the university. A worthy and neat idea. But the reality was not so neat. Colleges had to cope not only with immigration and poverty in two centuries, but with a rude citizenry clamoring for educational rights. Taking any student they could get, the early land-grant colleges incorporated high schools into their structures in order to advance students into college work. In the South after the Civil War, many newly formed black colleges either began as high schools or established high school departments. In the 1970s, higher education still struggles to do what high schools haven't done—to make American education reach some of its ideals. Though the causes today are more intractable, the "new" problems of open admissions are in many ways the old ones. A nation thinking of itself as new every decade still staggers under the burden of ignorance and promise, the burden of history.

Such noble purposes in a country officially in favor of education but at the same time deeply skeptical of it run not only into trouble but into comic situations. In the last century, voicing the antiintellectualism that still accompanies a lust for "education," many parents thought their children needed to learn little more than "the Bible and figgers." The present cry, "Why, these students shouldn't be in college!" —a lament that even I have muttered now and then—is old as the hills. In his *State Universities and Democracy*, Allan Nevins quotes a student in the Jacksonian era at Indiana Seminary, the forerunner of Indiana University. When asked if he had bought the proper books, the entering student spoke for other rural nineteenth-century students and for a few, alas, in schools today. "Books! I have never heern tell of any books! Won't these ones do, Master? This here's the Western Spellin' one—and this one's the Western Kalkelatur."

Although open admissions can be seen as part of a historical progression in American education, so many changes had occurred between its nineteenth-century beginnings and its sudden rebirth in New York City that its reincarnation at CUNY was a radical departure. By the early 1900s, state universities, with a fairly sound high school system to support them, had developed highly regarded professional and technical departments, serving, in a field such as engineering, the needs of an industrializing nation, while providing liberal arts programs. By the 1950s, in every state in the Union, at least one public-supported university had become selective in its admissions policy; and sometimes, as in Michigan, Wisconsin, and California, highly selective. Other colleges in the state systems had lower standards; almost but not quite everyone could get into them. Consistently elite, CUNY's senior colleges had become highly competitive in admission and highly conscious of their academic reputations. Two-year community colleges, which CUNY formed after World War II, took up the slack, and democratically offered further education to high school graduates with low averages and to those uncertain about their academic interests. Before World War II, entrance into some public-supported colleges was not difficult, but going to college at that time usually indicated a strong academic or professional interest.

The new open admissions policies carried with them an upsurge in college attendance and a new set of values. In 1960, only one third of American high school graduates went to college, but by 1974 more than half entered either two- or four-year institutions. A college education, like the high school diploma in earlier years, had become not only a means of mobility and a passport to white collar work, but a status symbol in a still antiintellectual but increasingly status-conscious country. Open admissions offered in remedial courses the help that former easy access to college didn't provide; easy access in the past had meant that droves of unprepared students, put into regular freshman courses, were flunked out after the first year. When, in 1970, the City University of New York became the only university to establish a categorical open admissions policy in a four-year college, it made remedial education of the unprepared student an urgent component of the policy. Adding extra work and time to college education and trying to do the work that high schools have failed to accomplish, the remedial courses in reading, math, and writing try to help the student catch up and perform college level work. At CUNY, and in its various forms elsewhere, open admissions has brought two impulses of American education into conflict: equality of educational opportunity vying with the urge for educational quality at every turn.

The third largest university in the nation, now consisting of eight separate community colleges, nine senior colleges, and a graduate school, CUNY ostensibly met in Open Admissions the needs of black and Puerto Rican minorities. But numerically as many or more whites, mostly of working-class background, benefited, though the official minorities made substantial gains. CUNY—the most important city-supported university in the United States—had, like leading state universities, become so competitive that, in spite of programs under way to include minorities, it was vulnerable to a policy change.

Before Open Admissions lowered the barriers to students with poor high school records, the senior colleges had an admissions grade requirement of 85—higher than for most private colleges. In 1976, the fiscal crisis of New York City brought a curtailment to Open Admissions and ended the older policy of free tuition. The requirement for admission was now raised to an 80 grade average, or a standing in the top third of a high school graduating class. The imposition of tuition for the first time in CUNY's 129-year history limited opportunities for many low-income students in spite of tuition aid. It was designed, as were the new entrance requirements, to reduce enrollment. As a result of massive faculty firings, class size increased, making remedial and regular instruction less effective. In the flush of affluence and social democracy in the early seventies, remedial classes had numbered fifteen or twenty students and thus allowed extensive individual help; today with sometimes thirty or more remedial students in a class, the slow and timid do not get the same attention, though tutoring and lab work outside of class do make up for some of the loss.

Although the SEEK program continues to bring a random selection of minority students into the four-year colleges, the new admissions policy theoretically limits future entrance of most blacks, Puerto Ricans, and low-income whites to community colleges. In practice, the new admissions policy has proved more flexible—and pragmatic; in the scramble to maintain enrollment, some of CUNY's four-year colleges have been able to admit new students with an average below 80. (A 75 or 80 average in a ghetto high school usually means undereducation and limited ability in language and math.) But flexible admissions, which could keep opportunities for minorities open, are threatened because budget cuts are being rigorously applied at those colleges. On the surface, access to community colleges might seem to assure continued Open Admissions as the university officially claims, but with some exceptions, remedial programing at community colleges is so thin as to be worthless. Too many graduates of community colleges, on transferring to four-year schools, have failed the latter's reading and writing placement tests to allow that official delusion much credence. Too much community college work is vocational—hotel keeping and lab work—valid for the marketplace but not necessarily for academic competence.

Given the choice of trying a senior college, the student himself had to meet the test of motivation, and by the act of entering, risk failure. Remedial courses, introduced at great expense, preparing him for the regular curriculum, could add a year or more to his college work and turn college into a five- or six-year challenge. Both the new freedom of Open Admissions and the old glory of free tuition proved the most expendable items in New York City's budget when the city found itself bankrupt. If Open Admissions at CUNY needed minor surgery, its heart was cut out in the budget cutting. Roughly half of CUNY's budget had been sustained by the city, half by the state. It was vulnerable to city budget cuts because the city had no actual constitutional obligation to support four-year colleges, and the state treated it as a rival to the growing State University—even though the state had increased its proportion of CUNY support. In the first crisis year CUNY's budget was cut more than that of any other city agency—$70 million. The schools also suffered huge faculty firings and a drop of 22 percent in enrollment. The noble idea of public higher education, a legacy of the previous century, fell under the dead weight of New York City.

The great challenge for Open Admissions was to bring respectable standards and decent opportunity into balance. Certainly, some failures were inevitable in its first years. At the same time, thousands of students, black and white, did master the remedial courses, continued in the regular curriculum, and received diplomas—even with honors. At York, in 1974, among the top graduates were an Open Admissions student with a *summa cum laude* in political science and a SEEK student with a *magna* in history. Both had been low-average high school graduates and required remedial courses.

Has Open Admissions been a success? A recent study showed that of all the students entering in 1970—except for those in the SEEK program—44 percent had been graduated five years later. Nationally, a little less than half of those entering college graduate in a similar period of time. The CUNY figures, of course, included all students, those who needed remediation and those who didn't. Open Admissions was effective with countless individuals who would not have been in college without it. Did it destroy standards, as its many opponents claimed it would? Certainly it made it easier for colleges to offer junk courses and purely vocational majors with fewer liberal arts requirements. The new student body was vulnerable to a lowering of requirements, brought about not by their admission to the college but by curriculum changes of the sixties, wrought by the crusade for "relevancy," and by the politicization of middle-class students.

As almost everywhere else, at CUNY English Composition became virtually the only requirement, as free choice was introduced in the humanities, social sciences, and sciences. While students had to take some courses in each of these areas, many of the offerings were weakened by an emphasis on the contemporary and the topical at the expense of intellectual substance. European and classical civilization were deemed "irrelevant," and with other basic college courses, were ignored as students rushed to register for courses in computer programming, the contemporary novel, or the like. Yet, despite suffering its own version of the national disease, in its remedial curriculum CUNY did teach people to write, read, and think—and did provide serious education, to those who would accept it. It did equip minorities to cope with the world.

In the first years of Open Admissions, every department was riven with conflict over how to "maintain standards" and educate the new student. With traditionalists in control of many departments, reformers who had an innovative approach toward remedial education were often the first to be fired when issues of reappointment and tenure arose. So great was the friction at City College that charges of misconduct were brought against a tenured professor in the History Department by leaders of an opposing faction. Yet, though reformers came and went, many of their ideas influenced the traditionalists. Adapting to the new realities, the traditionalists were able to influence the remedial curriculum in helpful ways.

In the early years of Open Admissions at York, the English Department fought bitter internal battles over minimal credit for remedial courses. The next battle was for a department-wide written essay exam to be given midway in the three-stage remedial sequence; it was instituted. The exam did show which students were ready to move on to the final remedial writing course, requiring a term paper. The exams were graded by other teachers as well as by the student's regular teacher, and the grades were not binding but advisory, helping to bring perspective to a teacher's final mark and getting him off the hook of personal sympathies. Finally, with no opposition in the English faculty, a postremedial written essay exam was established as a requirement for graduation. After reading one hundred such exams last year, the faculty was stunned, not by any failure of remediation, but by the conspicuous gain in clarity and grammar. Even the fifty students who failed wrote papers way above the level of entering students. They were failed on stiff standards—a wrong tense or a lousy verb agreement—standards we all felt should apply absolutely. It will not take much—perhaps their own review of the exam, perhaps tutoring, or even another writing course—for students to meet the final requirements of writing a clear, grammatically respectful paper. The truth is, with the faculty concurring on standards and students rising to meet them, Open Admissions was just learning to do its job well when it was halted.

Out of the 1976 plan to curtail enrollment came one reform upholding the work already begun in some of the colleges to raise standards. Beginning in September 1978, placement tests in writing, reading, and math—now given in most of the colleges to determine whether a freshman needs remediation—will become university-wide requirements. Students at the four-year colleges will have to pass the tests, either on entering or after remedial work, in order to move from sophomore to junior level. At the community colleges, students will not be allowed to transfer to a senior college without passing the tests, though they will still get the two-year degree regardless of test performance. The objective test in math should pose no problem. Though no multiple-choice reading test can give an accurate measurement of ability, and though an emphasis on reading tests is destructive to education, the twelfth-grade-level reading requirement may make this test valuable. The possibility of cultural bias will have to be considered, however, if blacks fail it in large numbers. The writing test, like the proficiency exam now given at York and at a few other colleges, will ask the student to respond with an organized essay of his own to some "stimulating" passage of contemporary interest and will bring an irrefutable strengthening of standards everywhere.

Presumably, students, if they can maintain passing grades and stay in college, can work and work until they pass the tests. But the tests have ramifications intended for use beyond CUNY itself. According to the university, the tests are "a signal to high school students and the schools themselves" to shape up on the basic skills.

Just as the presence and manifest needs of the nineteenth-century land-grant colleges, in Allan Nevins's phrase, "called the high school into being," so conceivably could tangible standards at CUNY and at other public universities call the high school back to work. If there are not absolute standards in colleges, there will not be standards anywhere. Open admissions and college remedial work are less a political response to the needs of minorities than a desperate solution to the failure of high schools to teach. Open admissions dramatizes the results, though not the fundamental causes, of the public school failure. Not only objective-test teaching contributes to the crisis that the university has been forced to relieve. So do teachers who are illiterate, who are fearful of students but secure in their jobs; undergraduate and graduate programs in education which teach rigid, uncreative method courses; state boards of education which certify teachers solely on the number of credits accumulated; and unions which protect teachers regardless of competence or suitability. The public cannot forever tolerate the disgrace in public education. Nor can the public university forever cope with the abdication of secondary school teaching. If it does nothing else, the university should demand that the public school system pay part of the huge remediation cost.

It is to emergencies that the democratic impulse in higher education, from the beginning to the present, has responded. However, neither the public nor the public university sees the need for remedial education as a permanent condition. But if minorities are not to be savagely pushed out of higher education, public schools will have to prepare far more of them for college work than it does now.

An old-fashioned toughness must meet with democratic fair play. Perhaps everywhere in the country no student should be admitted to college unless he can write an essay. Let's try that standard for one year and see what happens. Alas, the educational utopia does not exist in America.

Open Admissions, when it ran at full blast from 1970 to 1976, displayed all the curiosities of technologically oriented, upwardly mobile culture. More selective than it seemed, the policy encouraged students with a below-80 average to enter community colleges. In practice, however, any New York high school graduate who applied to a four-year City University college, whatever his grade, was admitted. In the senior colleges, half the entering freshmen had below-80 averages, while in community colleges 63 percent fell below 75. Actually, the grade average indicated very little, except where it had been obtained in a recognizably good high school; the diploma entitling a student to admission might have come from an academic school, a ghetto school with watered-down courses, or a trade school. The higher a student's average, the better his chances of admission to the college of his first choice.

Under Open Admissions, democracy worked by computer assignment, and the computer sent a set quota of low-average students to each institution. High-average students remained a majority at the older, prestigious four-year colleges—

Hunter, Queens, and Brooklyn—while most of the low-average students were dispersed to smaller, newer four-year schools—York, Lehman, John Jay, and Baruch. City College, situated on the edge of Harlem, the oldest of the colleges and the scene of a campus takeover, provided an exception to that rule by educating many low-average students.

Among its alumni City University can count not only the celebrated—Bernard Baruch, Felix Frankfurter, Jonas Salk —but the businessmen, lawyers, physicians, and teachers of a profoundly American city. However poor its students in the past, they came from cultures intact, families honoring learning, schools that prepared their graduates. Having become selective in the 1930s, City College was called a proletarian Harvard. In the post-World War II period, CUNY began to compete with private universities even more intensely than some public institutions for academic prestige. Offering high salaries to a few, but always relying on poorly paid graduate students and part-time faculty to do much of its teaching, the City University became a study in mixed American motives. Chartered as a public university by myth as well as deed, it inevitably yielded to the realities of a changing city in adopting an Open Admissions policy. But much of its faculty, though accepting Open Admissions in principle in the 1970s, was unprepared by experience and training for an onslaught of the poorly educated. Though younger faculty did much of the remedial teaching, older faculty members, sometimes hostile to the new student, often found enrollment in their specialties declining and found themselves facing tragic misplacement.

CUNY was in the throes of change that its own structure had not prepared it for. While it was embarking on Open Admissions, it was also instituting a separate graduate center to add to its academic prestige. If CUNY had been socially responsible first, and controlled by fiscal sanity, the graduate center might never have been built—and Open Admissions at that time of fiscal crisis might have been more viable. But CUNY was more than the "multipurpose university" made fashionable in the 1950s and early 1960s. It was an American contradiction, striving for the illusions of excellence, stooping to help the ignorant, in one grand gesture. Its social conscience had long preserved the American idea of free higher education for those who wanted it; it had helped the weak to stay in school instead of maintaining the Puritan democracy of the old state colleges that flunked them out without the help of remedial courses. If it ever had been possible to choose between its two heads, by the time of fiscal crisis it was too late. A graduate center boasting excellence couldn't be torn down, but vocational community colleges could be used as a form of Open Admissions.

Free tuition at CUNY, lasting more than a century, reflected the early idealism of public-supported higher education. Entering the twentieth century, the land-grant and state colleges kept the cost of college low by charging reasonable "fees" rather than direct tuition. But time, setting different priorities, and some indeterminable wearing down of the public spirit, had so eroded the free-tuition principle that by the 1970s the City University of New York was the only public institution of higher learning that preserved it. Ever since Governor Rockefeller built his State University and reluctantly imposed tuition there, CUNY had ironically been regarded as niggardly for not imposing it too. Actually, students at CUNY paid $110 a year in "fees." State and city had roughly split the costs of CUNY prior to the budget crisis, but now, with the city reducing its contribution and the state resisting an increase in its portion, tuition became the price for further state aid.

Partly a cosmetic, tuition appeased suburban sentiment while requiring state aid. In return for tuition, the state agreed to extend its tuition-assistance plan to needy CUNY students, whose numbers strained the program and brought about a reduction in the amounts available to them. The "special case" of a municipal university—and its unique purpose—boggle the logic of state criteria. State University students include relatively few students who work and go to college part time; but at CUNY the "emancipated" student —often an adult in his thirties—and the part-timer, working

as he goes to college, are the mainstays of academic achievement.

Free tuition had meant that city residents could get an
education at any age; under today's tuition requirements the
part-time student is not covered by tuition assistance. When
tuition was imposed, people working full time and taking
evening courses found they could not continue; parents who
were sending children to college and attending college themselves found they could not afford tuition for two generations, and dropped out.

Tuition became, finally, a device, not for sustaining the
university, but for cutting enrollment. Conceived as a political and psychological weapon by political strategists, the
imposition of tuition scared away thousands of potential
students. The true "saving" accomplished by imposing tuition was the loss of fifty thousand students in one year.
Tuition did not save money; it only shifted the burden,
slightly. For example, of the $8 million collected in tuition
at City College in 1976–77, $6.5 million came from state and
federal funds aiding students. Theoretically, this money
could have supported the continuance of free tuition, but due
to the political nature of federal, state, and local relationships, the federal government did not support a valuable
institution when local support faltered.

Representing lost educational opportunities for many,
the abandonment of a free-tuition policy also stood for a
loss of civic virtue. Free tuition engendered in generations
of CUNY graduates a sense of gratitude and civic obligation. For having been given a free high education, notable
CUNY alumni have often said that they want to return
to society what society gave them. In contrast, tuition aid
is a burden and a humiliation. It encourages resentment
and corrupts the citizenry. Tuition-aid applications ask
endless personal questions about family income. For many
blacks, questions about their father's occupation invite
feelings of worthlessness. One student told me, "I haven't
heard of my father for years. I'm forced to say he's
dead." Like applicants for welfare, financial-aid applicants

have to prove their eligibility. In order to do so they suffer an invasion of privacy. Because need is great, there is the pressure to withhold or falsify information. Those who do justify it with the excuse that "the rich cheat all the time." Free higher education offered an implicit lesson in democracy. Its loss is felt in more ways than one.

The maintenance of free public institutions is infinitely better for democracy than proliferating special aid programs —far better for New York's poor, for New York itself, if the federal government had been able to practice real socialism and support free higher education, as other western democracies do. Given free tuition, generations of New Yorkers have worked for the betterment of a city. While trust breeds trust, suspicion breeds suspicion, self-interest, and finally greed. It is not only the barrage of television advertising, not only the commercialism of society itself, but the stinginess and suspicion of investigatory government programs that give rise today to the deplorable cult of "looking out for number one." It is from that attitude that democracy in America may finally fall.

Free tuition and Open Admissions not only conferred trust and hope; they trained people to be more responsible parents, more productive citizens. The statement, so often heard from black students, that they were going to college so their children would get a better education, expresses how Open Admissions allowed one generation to advance the possibilities of the next. The immediate effect of the cutbacks was large. Tuition not only limited the opportunities of the poor; it also drove away the middle class.

Free tuition was one reason for middle-class families to stay in New York. The State University system, with the same $750–$900 tuition, and private colleges, with considerably higher costs, will become appealing alternatives to a budget-decimated City University. Already, budget cuts are so severe that the number of course offerings in some departments at CUNY is perilously slim. It is altogether possible that, like many public schools in New York now, CUNY will eventually become an aid station for the luckiest of the black poor, instead of the truly integrated experience it has so far been.

It was the politics of change, particularly of black power, that brought Open Admissions about. The civil rights movement, moving north, becoming militant, attached itself to a goal the public and the press lauded as worthy. While shoe leather at Selma, Alabama, and marches throughout the South had won civil rights in congressional legislation, clenched fists, threats, and the seizure of property wrested a victory from the largest public university in a northern city. And the university, meeting the pressure with Open Admissions, exercising its social responsibility, demonstrated the adaptability of institutions to change. But the urban political realities that brought Open Admissions to an end were mismanagement, helplessness, and greed.

Coinciding with the demand for educational rights in New York City was the demand by the service unions of sanitation workers, police, firemen, civil servants, and teachers for escalating fringe benefits and salaries. The crisis was cast in the 1960s when the Sanitation Workers' Union went on strike, and Governor Rockefeller, courting union support, refused Mayor Lindsay's request for the National Guard to keep the city clean. A city is spineless—and collective bargaining doesn't work—when municipal government has no power to protect the public interest. The power of organizational politics rules instead. Union leadership, to secure its internal position, asked for benefits beyond the expectations of its membership. Following the sanitation workers' victory, union after union, from firemen to CUNY faculty, pressed for increased benefits and won. At CUNY, the faculty union, the Professional Staff Congress, an affiliate of the American Federation of Teachers, came to power in the late 1960s because of inequitable city policy: half the faculty was paid handsomely with full benefits and salary; the other half was paid by the hour, with no benefits at all. Too late to have an effect on the present, the New York State legislature in 1976 reduced city pension contributions slightly—for future employees, when and if hired. Unions made a theoretical concession in tying future cost-of-living increases either to a cut in fringe benefits or to an increase in productivity, an agreement still to be tested. And, in an inevitable act of poetic justice, the unions have found it necessary to loan the city huge sums from their pension funds in order to keep the city afloat and a minimal work force employed.

Just as the university itself was building its glittering graduate center, so was the city off on its fringe-benefits spree. While the City of New York never set priorities between the needs of Open Admissions and the needs of other city agencies, it did yield to Open Admissions with an idealism suggesting its social worth.

The middle-class subsidies, climbing in union contract after contract to salary and employee benefits higher than in any other municipality, excluded the principle of employee contribution, common in private industry still. Noncontributory health and pension programs had become a vogue, promising a bankrupt New York. Although a reduction in fringe benefits would not have gotten the city out of its fiscal hole, such a cut would have made the pit less deep. In the CUNY budget, reduced from $539 million to $470 million in 1976, $100 million, or almost a quarter of the operating costs, went into fringe benefits—$30 million more than the cut itself. If, as a lone city councilman urged, city pension costs had been deferred, thousands of employees could have kept their jobs. And perhaps Open Admissions might have been salvaged. Unions could have bartered a pension deferment or a fringe-benefit adjustment for the saving of jobs, while keeping the existing pensions intact and inviting voluntary contributions. But instead of leadership from the unions, instead of public-interest leadership from governor or mayor or any other politician, the self-destructive course of New York City, which ultimately determined the fate of Open Admissions, continued. Thousands of city employees, including City University faculty, have since been thrown out of work, and thousands more students will be squeezed out of higher education in the future to bail the city out of its debt. Obviously large social forces—the welfare load of the poor and the move of the middle class and industry from city to suburb—joined with New York's own political mistakes to bring on the fiscal disaster. New York's fall may spell the end of the myth of cities as places where the poor do rise, where hard work in classroom and on the job is rewarded.

Seven years before the city itself—and an American educational dream in particular—was brought to its knees came the spring of democratic expectations. In May of 1969, as American campuses erupted in protests against the Vietnam war and shouts for social justice at home, militant black students at CUNY seized the mood of unrest and waged their successful revolution. Leading a list of "nonnegotiable demands" was a call for an immediate open admissions policy. Because the subject of minority education was in the air, because existing programs like SEEK were insufficient, open admissions was already a part of a City University Master Plan, a blueprint to come into effect in 1975. But these demonstrators were not prepared to wait. With a mature, centralized leadership and a clear purpose in mind, they forced—through the demonstrations—the beginning of open admissions in the fall of 1970. As it turned out, 1975 would have been too late.

The demonstrations began at City College, close to Harlem. There, a university-wide organization called BLACK occupied buildings and closed down the campus. Brooklyn College, where I was teaching at the time, was also the scene of BLACK militance. One of its leaders at Brooklyn College, in the forefront of the sit-ins, forums, and marches, was a student of mine in a writing class. When I first saw his name on the class card—Curtis Liberty—I was taken aback. Could a name descended from the slavery of the South be so defiant? What southern legacy would have bestowed Liberty? Perhaps there was a lineage of protest or a name changed somewhere with due respect to freedom.

Lithe in movement, straight in posture, as if in this new era of the Malcolm X legend and Black Panther breakfasts a weight had been lifted from his shoulders, he stood for the style of his generation—grace was a purpose. Tall, spare in build, slightly hollow-cheeked, he was a natural aristocrat. If you saw him walking in a hallway, you saw a man who knew where he was going; but when he stopped to talk, everything else about him stopped too. In character as well as language, style is spirit showing itself. Spirit he had, in his writing and his manner.

The term before, he had taken the same remedial course with a rules-and-regulations teacher and had failed. His contempt for her was restrained and short-spoken. Once he was allowed to use his thoughts and interests in his writing, his grammar improved, and he had no trouble getting ahead. Before entering college through the SEEK program, he had been at a trade school, learning to run a lathe. SEEK, then in its second year, was the wedge for social change, and thus provided the manpower for the student demonstrations.

The revolution was around us. During the demonstrations the acting college president had said he would meet with black militants to discuss their demands, but not in the presence of their allies, the white protesters who, joining in the free-for-all protest, had branded him a "pig" and burned a papier-mâché pig in effigy. A fair-minded, urbane, and humane man, a former chairman of the English Department, he would have found the pig ceremony offensive no matter who the pig had represented. "His feelings are just hurt because they called him a 'pig,' " Liberty asserted in class. "He should know who he is. Lots of times people call me a Negro and I don't close up. They can call me that all they want, but I know who I am." I was dumbfounded that he should consider "pig" and "Negro" equally defamatory. But the climate allowed, even with Liberty's sense of distinctions, for such confusions. "Black," which had recently come into currency, I now know, as everybody should, is preferable because blacks, not whites, chose it.

Campus issues were a good subject, a good way of getting students involved in the act of writing. In one paper Liberty wrote of a demonstration in Albany and described New York

State as "run on hate." When I questioned the charge, he had the answer of a gentleman. "I've got some information you haven't. Let's talk about it later." The paper told of SEEK students going to the capital on "a day right for hate," to protest the usual threats of cuts in the SEEK budget. On the bus the students had a picnic lunch, chiefly chicken, and had started to sing. When they arrived in Albany, they didn't demonstrate strongly enough, in Liberty's opinion, but had lolled around in the sun. With a nice play on American idiom, he had entitled the paper "Too Much Chicken."

Even when the campus protests in which he was involved kept others away, Liberty rarely missed class. Though he was distressed by revolutionary laxity, he knew how to get away from the world too. When asked after spring vacation to render an impression holding to his mind, he wrote:

> The sea is a wonder to behold. The way the sun strikes the ocean waves and causes them to glide like diamonds in a store front window. The sea can talk, it roars as it smashes against the shore. The mind can get lost in the vastness of the sea. Your thoughts are like grains of sand, your worries are like pebbles being eaten by the jaws of timeless eternity. Man has conquered many things, but man has yet to conquer the sea.

He could put a "jaw" on eternity and avert a cliché. He was an original, many-sided fellow. One day in class he offered a phrase from his ocean indicting poverty—"the psychological death all around you." Once he told of white girls who took notes all through an evening lecture by the psychologist Kenneth Clark. "Why do they want to take all that down for? He was just talking from one human being to another." Much of America, from its store windows to its hope for humanism, was inside him. When he talked, the words flew forth as from a breathless typewriter, a merry ring coming out every once in a while.

The demonstrations weren't far under way at Brooklyn College before BLACK began sporting a Security Guard, of which Liberty was a member. The members of the Guard carried ominous canes with carved handles—books in one hand, the cane in the other. The Security Guard, Liberty patiently told me, was purely defensive. He said that members of the Jewish Defense League had shown up armed with clubs at a BLACK meeting. At a turbulent college forum, designed to air demands and let off steam, the Security Guard showed its colors. After a speaker for BLACK had made an abusive speech, a fight had broken out between a black man and a white. From all sides of the auditorium came strapping black figures, running down the aisles; one of them was Liberty. I thought the big fight had come. But the Security Guard separated the two men and kept order.

At the forums the black students sat in a bloc in the middle of the auditorium, and whenever a BLACK speaker took the microphone or finished a speech they raised clenched fists and shouted, "Power to the People." The fists went up by the hundreds, the cry rocked the hall. I thought I was in Cuba —or watching a newsreel of the 1930s in which there was one antifascist, myself, not cheering. The college's acting president gave a civilized talk on the considerable effort the college had made to bring minorities into college. But the drama —and some of the urbanity—was all on the other side.

Liberty came into class one day and gave the only gentle clenched fist I've seen. Seeing a "brother," he smiled; and his hand hanging down, clenching his fist at his side, he said "Power" quietly. Like his contemporaries, he was a student and disciple of Malcolm X, a militant who would allow for the possibilities of a Mecca. There would be no turning marches around, as Martin Luther King had done, because the police had refused a permit. Like other students, he criticized black Christianity for telling black folk to sing and wait. His mother was a devout Baptist—and he was a good son—but he represented, conspicuously, the generation gap occurring in his world.

In May he was arrested at dawn, dragged from his family's house in Bedford-Stuyvesant, and locked up on Welfare Island for three days. After a rally, the shouts in the auditorium had been followed by windows being smashed and fires breaking out in bathrooms. There was no evidence against anyone, but plainclothes policemen observing the public meetings had collected the names and taken pictures of the BLACK leaders. They were charged with conspiracy to commit arson and violence, and bail was set by a Brooklyn judge at an extravagant $12,000 for each of eleven poverty-stricken students. The judge and a Brooklyn district attorney, not the college administration, were responding to a fearful constituency. The college administration, sensitive to its students and the severity of bail, petitioned successfully to reduce it to $3000. The generation gap closing, his mother gave a speech at a Bedford-Stuyvesant rally to help raise the bail. Perhaps the combustion was spontaneous, perhaps it came from fringe groups on either side, perhaps it was organized from the outside; but it wasn't the work of Liberty. A safe year later, the charges against the students were quietly dropped.

Coming into class after three days in jail, Liberty had a new hardness in his voice, an unfamiliar stiffness in his walk. He talked, however, not as a victim but as a social critic. The police had been buffoons rather than brutes. They had searched his room for any book by a Chinese or Russian writer. They appeared solemn whenever reporters were around, but joked about the arrests when alone with their prisoners. He was distressed by the conditions on Welfare Island. The food was terrible, but the prisoners had to eat or starve. One prisoner he had talked to was going mad because of trial delay and lack of counsel. Liberty was moved by injustice.

He presided over inner and outer complexities very well. He was in touch with himself, in control. But in another student, the president of BLACK, militancy had sprung out of a cashmere sweater and torn it to shreds. Coming to Brooklyn College under an Equal Opportunities program, Raymond Williams had been in a class of mine two years earlier. Meek, mild, and middle class, he usually dressed in well-pressed slacks and a tweed coat, or sometimes a sweater. Prolonging a conference on his work, he had shown me snapshots of his brother in army uniform, of his nicely dressed mother, of his house with a garden in front; and in all this middle-class virtue made a plea for approval and friendship. Two months later, wrapped in an African *dashiki*, he had stormed into a faculty meeting discussing broader admissions policies and had hurled insults and obscenities at the stunned teachers. A year later, he rose at the college forum in his *dashiki* uniform and raised two clenched fists before delivering a speech full of antiimperialist epithets that might have been written for Ho Chi Minh. However callow an assault on the capitalist system, it was more fluent than any paper he had done in class—and may have been plagiarized, supplied by a central organization behind the university-wide demonstrations. "Power to the People," the black claque shouted whenever he came to a pause, looked up, and waited. When he sat down, the flashbulbs popped. He spread his legs apart and raised two clenched fists, a little Nkrumah, a little Castro. In class I sought to counter the perversion of power, and told how fanaticism, from the French guillotine to the Stalin purges, had displaced the original idealism of revolutions. Liberty listened respectfully. "We'll be different," he said.

The arrests included the speechmaker and came just as the BLACK membership was seriously considering jettisoning Williams because of authoritarian tendencies. But the arrest made him a martyr; he was confirmed in power. After his release from prison, he was surrounded by his own bodyguards. One afternoon I encountered him, dressed inconspicuously, for once alone, in the college quadrangle. Stretching out his hand, calling my name, he smiled like a little boy who wanted reassurance. "I hope you know what you're doing," I said. He said he did. I could not be gentle with him if I wanted to make any dent in his armor at all and, wanting to dig out the self-righteousness in his new posture, chose an abstraction, slightly self-righteous itself. "Don't think you're the only angels," I said.

"The only angels?" He doubled over and laughed the laugh of a devil.

A professed Catholic when he had been in my class, Williams had been working in a community-action program and was frustrated by the inadequacies of the antipoverty program. But beyond social frustration, ferocity had been waiting to spring from some private den within him. Unlike Liberty, who knew how to look inward, I doubt that Williams's temperament or his circumstances had ever allowed him to. Certainly his writing in the class had been impersonal. Like the snapshots he had shown me, his life had been a pretense of stability. The door of illusion had been sprung, and when the lion of anger emerged, he couldn't control it. He took the revolution as the children of the affluent took a psychedelic drug.

At this college of fifteen thousand students there had been a cold distance between the whites and blacks who were there for the first time in significant numbers because of the expansion of SEEK. Perhaps I imagined it, but it looked to me as if some whites elbowed blacks aside in the crowded stairwells. When I asked my class how they liked the college, there was a frozen silence and a few grimaces. One girl told me a white girl she had known in high school would not speak to her here. A husky young man said that when he had played on his high school football team, the whites would not block for him. No white ran interference for him here either.

The spring protests, feeding on many grievances, forced the white students to look at their nonwhite contemporaries. While many whites were indifferent to, or annoyed by, the demonstrations—"Do they have the right to call off classes?" some blacks as well as whites asked—two minds began to approach each other in the sleepy afternoons. On the grassy Brooklyn quadrangle, the sun shining through the new leaves, the ground strewn with leaflets, whites stood in clusters around blacks explaining their case. Faced with brick, white-trimmed architecture, the campus was a reproduction of the colonial American quadrangle, now become a Union Square. At the center of one circle stood a supple young black, luminous in eye, speaking in a soft voice. No violence had occurred at Brooklyn College, he said, compared to the violence visited on blacks by the ghetto every day. It was a good point stretched further. This wasn't his country, he said; he just happened to be here. Then a student with an Eastern European accent, coming to the defense of America, said with belligerence that he shouldn't talk that way. The black student smiled, didn't yield a point, just continued his song. Soon the young immigrant apologized and said he didn't want to start a fight.

Another afternoon, seeing an Orthodox Jewish student of mine appraising the outdoor gathering, I brought him over to talk with a Puerto Rican student who had been active in the demonstrations. In Juan, cherubic, smiling, serious about his college opportunity, I had always sensed the desire to please me—I had been his adviser in an Equal Opportunity program—and anyone else in authority. But his embarrassing bootlicking was gone now. He began telling the Jewish student what open admissions could mean. To admit, regardless of race, "all the poor" who were high school graduates was the right and practical thing to do. The Orthodox boy, who was quietly fascinated by his secular college, stood back with a dreamy look I had only seen a hint of in his face before and said, "It's a beautiful idea."

In the first years of Open Admissions, the "beautiful idea" probably worked to the benefit of more whites than blacks. Although black participation rose sharply as Open Admissions continued, all along it brought low-income whites, chiefly Catholics, into the once predominantly Jewish student body. While the percentage of whites shrank from 80 to 60 percent of total number of students in the nine senior and eight two-year colleges, their actual numbers rose in a swollen enrollment. The percentage of blacks increased from 14 to 27 percent; Puerto Rican student numbers rose from 6 to 14 percent.

SEEK, which preceded Open Admissions in the senior colleges and now outlasts it, began in 1967 with 1450 students and rose to an enrollment of 10,000, mostly black, but with thousands of Puerto Ricans and a few whites. Growing every year for a decade, funded by the New York State legislature (half state and half city money)—$29 million a year at its height, $27 million now—SEEK is one antipoverty program begun in the sixties that has lasted. Unlike Open Admissions, it has a clear constituency—and in black and Puerto Rican political leaders in the legislature, the clout to survive. Reaching out to the ghetto student, attempting in its programs to leap over decades of denial, SEEK is open admissions with aim.

In the original requirements for SEEK, drawn up in legislation of 1966, students had to be residents of the city's designated "poverty areas" and had to fall below a maximum income level. In those days, before white ethnic groups placed a claim on antipoverty money, the two requirements were deemed enough to prove students "educationally disadvantaged." But as charges of preferential treatment rose, pressure mounted to make "educational disadvantage" the one qualification. "Poverty area" was dropped, and income level and "educational disadvantage" were left to determine what they could. Students with a below-80 average and a low income now qualified. SEEK became a miniature Open Admissions, but without the latter's latitude and advantages. A rumored influx of Hasidic Jews, left out of "poverty areas" but qualifying under the income level, didn't materialize because their excellent talmudic educations in Yeshivas hardly left them educationally poor. SEEK is, has been, and probably always will be a program primarily for blacks and Puerto Ricans, with room for the random inclusion of others.

Bureaucracy has always given SEEK a hard time. Originally, its candidates were recommended by churches, community agencies, or schools—and then individually interviewed. But political pressures from the agencies to take their candidates made fair selection difficult. The Board of Higher Education, dispersing Open Admissions candidates to different colleges by computer selection, concluded that SEEK students should be subject to the same fishbowl. Under this procedure, the computer was used for candidate selection—not for mere assignment. One out of nine SEEK applicants made it to college, not through any test of motivation, but through sheer chance. Open Admissions students had to bear whatever costs they incurred at college, and now pay tuition; consequently they had to be reasonably motivated. SEEK applicants could be lured by a monthly stipend, a book allowance, and now complete tuition aid, pooled from various funds. Traditionally, in such a scholarship program, motivation has been weighed, but, like the random selection process itself, in SEEK motivation was a product of chance. Among those left out by the computer, there may have been candidates of great promise, while some of those admitted may have been cruelly misled. Motivation could still be determined by interviews—if the Board of Higher Education would allow them. The board has not only dropped interviews but ceased requiring recommendations.

SEEK directors are not happy with this admissions policy; they fought in vain for selection by interview against a bureaucracy bent on its numb ways. The lower success rate of SEEK—19.1 percent of its 1970 entrants had graduated after six years, as compared to 44 percent of all other 1970 entrants who had graduated after five years—is partly the result of greater poverty among SEEK students, partly the legacy of discrimination felt especially in the inferior ghetto public school, but it is also the result of computer selection. If motivated students had been selected, perhaps by interview, a higher rate of graduation might have been secured from candidates of the same poverty, the same inferior public school education. In effect, screening takes place in the remedial courses. Among those surviving the early courses, the graduation rate increases. SEEK's success has to be measured by those who wrought the greatest gains from the program; these include not only the graduates, but also students who transfer to community colleges, students who emerge—from whatever time they have spent in the program—better able to master their lives.

Operating separately in each of the senior colleges, SEEK offers counseling from a largely black staff—and remedial courses taught by teachers hired for that purpose. Whereas Open Admissions students were taught by traditional faculty, the SEEK teacher, incurring his academic colleague's skepticism, often didn't have a Ph.D. but indicated some capacity for teaching the unprepared. An English professor at Brooklyn College, director of SEEK when it started, suggested that in teaching the semiliterate, we might "learn how to teach English." But while SEEK has had some influence on teaching, it has been fought by traditionalists, savagely and softly—the degree varying according to the college.

Today, reaping the consequences of bureaucratic blunders, SEEK is under attack not only for its low graduation figures but also for "financial irregularity." The New York State Commission of Investigation accuses SEEK of giving funds to "clearly ineligible students for whom the program was not intended." The irony of American government, especially in regard to antipoverty programs, is as follows: The law is so hamstrung with restrictions and qualifications that the program is doomed to break some aspect of the complex rules. In SEEK's case, the income restrictions for eligible students are so complicated—involving not only the student but his family, who may not, in fact, help him with a proportional share of total family income—that inevitably some worthy low-income students turn out, after admission, to be technically ineligible. The clear fact that worthy low-income students have been helped is lost sight of in the state investigation. And so, due to the ever-remaining political opposition, a scandal is made out of a public service. America must become more sophisticated about the use of public money. Billions of dollars of waste are tolerated in defense spending; billions wasted and unnoticed in private enterprise. If this country were committed to its principles of helping the poor to help themselves, then a bit of "financial irregularity" in antipoverty efforts such as SEEK would be tolerated, perhaps corrected without penalty to the poor, rather than exploited.

The low graduation figure and "financial irregularity" conspire to strengthen all the forces critical of SEEK. College administrations, while approving the program in principle, are now even more jealous of SEEK's separate budget, which has remained virtually intact due to the political power of the black and Puerto Rican caucus in the state legislature. But, armed with superficially persuasive criticism, those opposed to SEEK can now work from within to weaken the program and divert its funds. Responding to criticism, the chancellor of the City University now proposes that the separate SEEK budget be absorbed into each college's total budget, with the president of each college having the authority to determine how the money is to be spent. Such a proposal, which may come to pass in one form or another, would reduce counseling services to SEEK students in need of the good counseling SEEK provides; it would make it impossible for SEEK to hire a separate faculty, geared to the needs of its special students; and it would dump those promising students who have encountered exceptional difficulties in the past into the relatively indifferent mainstream of undergraduate life. SEEK, which was designed to ease its students into the mainstream of education via remedial courses, won't even be able to do that. SEEK may ultimately become a sink-or-swim financial aid program. And, like many worthwhile and effective antipoverty programs of the 1960s, SEEK will be called a failure when, in reality, only the state's policy was a failure.

In spite of bureaucratic blunders, the law of human potential has allowed SEEK to work wonders. In its minority-student classes, SEEK grants a touch of separatism as a way of making integration work later. "If I go into a class right away with kids from better high schools," a SEEK student once said, "I feel I may be dumber than the kid sitting next to me and don't open my mouth. After a year in a SEEK class, I can go into any classroom and speak for myself." The separate classes do build the student's confidence—partly because of the approach of the SEEK teacher, partly because minority kids are conspicuously more comfortable and expressive with each other.

SEEK has developed more than confidence among its students. Many have moved out of remedial courses and onto the Dean's List. Two thousand students supported by SEEK have graduated. A bank executive, a sociology instructor at

Howard University, a Phi Beta Kappa law student, a medical student are among its boasts. Sending more secure citizens into the world as businessmen, teachers, health workers, parents, SEEK is training a new urban leadership.

The black consciousness of which students spoke—and wrote—so freely in the year of social revolution, has worn itself down. But in my class other troubles, painfully private, demonstrated a unity among the poor. A white and a black student had been thrown out of their homes for the same reason. Their fathers were angry at them for going to college rather than to work. Still I barged on—a do-good liberal trying to thrash writing out of their consciousness, from whence it had sprung the year before.

"Black, black, black, that's all they hear, in sociology, in history, in English," a black counselor told me. A young man in his late twenties came up and said he couldn't write the paper I had assigned on Frederick Douglass's description of the brutality of slavery. "I know all that, and I don't want to be reminded," he explained. I switched anthologies, and he found Thoreau's "Life Without Principle," a difficult essay, easy, and went on to write a fine term paper on *Walden.* At the end of the term he said, "Your method is the best," but neither of us could name it.

I had been saved in time. Some students, painfully aware of racism, its history and its legacy, find James Baldwin's "Notes of a Native Son," or other reading exposing them to racism's wounds, unbearable to read. I've learned to offer a choice, and to allude to black history, not to force it on students. In 1972, one student, a girl from Manhattan with a precise black consciousness and lovely manner, expressed dissatisfaction with a paper on Richard Wright. "That's all I seem able to write. It's the same old black business." A year later she wrote a fine term paper on F. Scott Fitzgerald. In that class I had skated toward the disaster of black issues again—who wants to be cast as a victim of history? There were requests to read something other than the anthology *Black Voices.* "We're all right now," the girl said. "We know who we are." When I mentioned black pride in a 1977 SEEK class, an eighteen-year-old girl said, in a stunning rebuff to black issues, "Oh that. That was before we were born."

Many of my students at York College, and that young lady in particular, are from Queens and enjoy some of its provincial pleasures. Springfield Gardens, for instance. Their identity rests in a church group, a basketball court, a garden apartment. At the large city colleges, especially in Manhattan, there may be more political awareness among SEEK students. Yet, think that you are done with black consciousness and a Muslim will be in your midst. Furthermore, he will wear a tweed coat and a button-down collar; and after you have discovered him, in an innocent discussion, by suggesting that fanatics have existed in every religious movement from Abraham to Calvin to Elijah Muhammed, after hitting his nerve center and bringing him to a doctrinaire defense, you will find him an affable fellow capable of writing wonders. Even as it sinks into history, black pride has done its work. It no longer has to be proclaimed. "It's time we stopped blaming the white man," a student said in 1977, voicing one new mood. "We should regain what has been stripped from us—the integrity, the hard work—and put it to use constructively."

Under new conditions of denial, black pride returns in a steady voice. In the 1977 class in which the girl had spoken her innocence, an articulate young man, a Vietnam veteran who had never written much in his life, acknowledged in a paper the civil rights gains of the last decade. "But there are segments of white America which have regressed, remained static, and refused to change their ways." Taking the American Indian as a target of prejudice, he wrote:

Nixon's trickery is symbolic of the history of this nation. Two-faced and forked tongued are two characteristics of America which have existed since the establishment of this country. They are not exclusive experiences of the red man, but have and are still experienced by minorities and people of color. You've heard of slight of *hand?* America is slight of tongue. Time after time America has failed or fallen short in keeping its promises. America has, continually, shown its incapability of enforcing the constitution or laws of the justice system when it comes to minorities or people of color. Why? I'm not sure, but I believe it is because white America enjoys the advantages and comfort of a white controlled country. In a white controlled country whites set their own standards which the rest of the country must follow. If blacks and other minorities were to have power in government or were heads of big businesses, whites would be forced to follow their standards. For example, if companies and businesses are controlled by whites, they can hire their relatives and other whites. By doing this they keep harmony among themselves, sharing the same values. But if blacks were to take control, whites would feel that blacks would do what they have done, hire their own kind and set their own standards. Therefore, black control would diminish the power of whites, upsetting their values and standards. To correct this misconception the white man has of the black man, a better understanding of each other's cultural background, and each other's wants and needs is a must. I believe this would help remove the barrier that separates the races.

Racism in America is not dead, but very much alive. The only difference between racism in the past, in the South, and racism today, is racism in the past was overt racism and today it is covert racism. America has shifted her racism and discrimination to the North, in recent years, as we have seen in the busing protests in Boston. The North, as well as the rest of the nation, discriminates against minorities in its hiring and firing practices. Minorities are the last hired and first fired, especially in today's recession, and particularly in the big cities like Los Angeles and New York. When the governor or mayor wants to save money, the first thing they do is cut the educational and training programs created especially for minorities and the poor. . . .

The writer of the paper, who wore the mantle of black pride, who in an earlier time would have been a political militant, was a veteran glad to be out of a military he despised, but so turned off by society that he wasn't interested in public stances. The sixties, drawing on the past, had inspired hope in the face of an unpopular war and urban injustice. He was enjoying some of that decade's victories but had none of its optimism, its sense of possibilities. During the presidential campaign, he expressed surprise that I should wonder why he was not registered to vote. He would be an excellent citizen. Exhausted, disgusted by what he had seen, he gave his energy to his college courses.

The subtle insights and forceful complaint of his paper, when read aloud to the class, met with class pride. The less articulate admired it; it spoke for them. The imposition of tuition, as the paper hinted, strikes black CUNY students as a racial attack. While their predecessors in SEEK fought for Open Admissions for others, there is no sign yet of what may be an inevitable push, sometime, somewhere, to restore it. When the curtailment of Open Admissions was announced, and hearings were held, there were demonstrations, a few of them huge but orderly, a few small but rough. Speakers on sound trucks and at bull horns once again marshaled the militant rhetoric of the sixties. In a high-pitched chorus, Puerto Rican girls from Hostos Community College, which was merged into another community college, chanted a refrain for the chancellor of CUNY: "Kibbee you be liar/ we set your ass on fire." Such cheerleading helped preserve Hostos's bilingual Spanish/English program in a new structure. In limiting Open Admissions, the Board of Higher Education took the calculated risk, proved right, that students were too complacent to raise a row. But the student demonstrations were only short of the 1969 mood—partly because the fiscal crisis was so apparent, partly because the change in admission standards was lost in a more controversial proposal to close several colleges. As many whites of the sixties have shifted from political activism, so many blacks, sometimes more from gains than losses, have retreated into personal struggles.

Begun by black pressure, benefiting whites as well, Open Admissions did reach a quiet triumph of integration. Unlike public school integration, the wide integration of CUNY colleges did not provoke serious racial incidents. At the beginning, subtle hostility was there, in the distance kept between the races, in complaints from black students about being slighted by whites. Into the early seventies, separatism was clear in solid blocs of blacks at cafeteria tables, solid blocs of whites, with a no-man's land in between. But by 1974, the gap seemed to be narrowing. Blacks and whites talked together in hallways. And friendships were initiated. Much of the tension has gone. Better still, integration has gained a real and human face where student leaders gather. In student government, middle-class white students from all-white sections of Queens become boosters of black student leaders; black student leaders, needing white support, come to know and like those who give it. The exchange is not merely political but also leads to traditional college camaraderie—coming out of shared tasks, shared trials, shared celebrations. On the college newspaper, and in other organizations, blacks and whites lead a college life together. One white senior wrote in a paper appraising his Open Admissions experiences: "I made a veritable collage of myself. I shucked the ethnic smugness of the Italian Club and sought out other people, other races. I ate falafel with David Levy, drank Schnapps with Franz Troppenz, ate souvlaki with Jimmy Zarvos and danced Merengue with Chantale Blanco. As I come to an end at York I can say the greatest thing I learned is that humanity is greater than the sum of its individual parts."

Rightfully wary of the world, a black graduate might not be as jubilant in his appraisal of Open Admissions. But he would have found an openness and an opening he had not expected. While society made good in one aspect of education, blacks still have to wait on the improved education of whites to gain a full measure of humanity. The white student's celebration of Open Admissions indicates its success in breaking down in varying degrees the greatest barrier to opportunity for blacks—white prejudice. That success, possible only in situations where blacks and whites come to know each other as individuals, creates a new American climate, a spirit of integration that may someday break down job and housing barriers.

Teaching at CUNY is the only way I've become a citizen of New York, this great Jewish, southern city. One of my former students, an Orthodox Jew, looking up from beneath his fedora when we met by chance on the subway, greeting me cordially after many years, asked me if I was still "so liberal." When I said yes, he said he was too, and asked where I was teaching. "I should have known," he moaned, "that you would be teaching in the SEEK program."

In the educational boom of the sixties and early seventies, two notions got loose: that everyone should go to college and that a college degree assured a good job. Such sentimental thinking erased all traces of nineteenth-century skepticism of college education. The last century celebrated the self-made man. Mark Twain, who never went to college, coined a characterization that must have pleased his contemporaries (and ought still to please us): "Training is everything. The peach was once a bitter almond; cauliflower is nothing but cabbage with a college education." Neither Abraham Lincoln, nor Henry James, nor Harry Truman were college graduates. Generally, it was the sons of the self-made men who first went to college. Thoreau maintained that he learned nothing valuable at Harvard; and a century later Robert Frost, a sore fellow, left Harvard in disgust. Both, of course, were well-educated men—self-educated. And it is self-education that schools should inspire. The encouragement of self-education is still the highest call of college, even while it engages in the world's work by offering vocational opportunity. Economic advance, without continued spiritual and intellectual growth, will ultimately impoverish Americans. The passport out of poverty that education at CUNY offers to many blacks is not worth the deposit if the education teaches only skills.

American colleges have for a long time been turned toward the world and used for utilitarian as well as for high-minded academic purposes. In theory, American education has taken the Greek idea of education for citizenship away from Plato, away from its class-conscious implementation in Europe, and applied it to a whole people. By abandoning history in schools today we fail the theory altogether. But pure education has long since given way to modified pragmatism. In the late nineteenth century, science and industry having become powerful, the elective system was introduced by Harvard's President Charles Eliot and became the rule in American colleges, weakening the grip of the classics and making it possible, through elective choice, for colleges to offer educations that could lead directly to jobs and serve the practical needs of American society. The curriculum yielded to such worldly subjects as engineering, economics, and business administration.

After World War II, specialization having made science and the humanities remote from each other, general education courses, again a Harvard innovation, sought to offer a common body of liberal arts knowledge in the first college years. All colleges, until the upheaval of the late 1960s, held to basic requirements—courses in the humanities, the social sciences, and the natural sciences. Only after basic requirements were completed could a student major in accounting. But the demand for relevance did away with such requirements in many colleges; and into the gap came the trend courses in women's studies, in sexual awareness, in the plight of minorities—offered to meet loose humanities requirements. Majors even more vocational than their pre-1960s predecessors were introduced as well. A new health major at York trains students to work in various community agencies dealing with air and water pollution, heroin addiction and venereal disease. As new vocational programs are introduced and old liberal arts requirements vanish, colleges teeter on the line of becoming trade schools. A health major might bring the student perspective as well as technical skills, if it required a student to study a history of epidemics and the response of societies throughout history to health problems. With such a perspective, health technicians would surely be better prepared to cope with the new and the unusual. But attention to the past is usually left out of the new vocational programs.

A lady I admired greatly was forced to go back to college to get an AB degree because New York law will soon require it of all full-fledged nurses. She so resented the vocational program she was advised to take that she hid away in literature and art courses. The AB requirement for a "nurse" is undoubtedly the work of the nursing and educational lobbies in state legislatures. Nurses with an AB will not be better nurses unless colleges become nursing schools.

In spite of all the good education diligent students still get for themselves, we have come to use education as an instrument of measurement itself. Those who have a college degree may use it to feel superior to those without one. Such feeble status labeling should revolt us. If we were honest and taught decently at all levels, if we recognized a diversity among people and removed from college the load of respectability, if we insisted that college be a ladder for the mind and the spirit, we might approach W. E. B. Du Bois's humanistic ideal of education. "And the final product of our training," he wrote in 1900, "must neither be a psychologist nor a brick mason, but a man. And to make men we must have ideals, broad, pure, and inspiring, ends of living—not sordid money-getting, not apples of gold. The worker must work for the glory of his handiwork, not simply for pay; the thinker must think, for truth, not fame."

Under Open Admissions, adults especially took their education seriously. Before tuition was imposed, mothers retired from family responsibilities, fathers holding full-time jobs, secretaries, policemen, firemen, and small businessmen enrolled for education of their minds. They used college for self-education; they recognized, by flocking to humanities courses, that education was for far more than a job, that it was for living an interesting life. Some came for enrichment in a few courses, others for enrichment and a degree. Until Open Admissions ended, the urban four-year college had become for them, as well as for many who were younger, a realization of a dream. At the 1977 York College commencement the two oldest graduates were seventy-one and seventy-two years old, the younger a handsome black man with a fringe of gray hair, the older a black lady who looked only about forty. When each walked off the stage, wearing cap and gown, degree in hand, the audience of faculty, students, and parents rose to applaud, to celebrate this human triumph. For them, and thousands of others, college had become a fulfillment of life in America that no other opportunity could provide.

For a few years more, CUNY graduating classes will include some older students who began the program when it was tuition-free. For many older students the dream of a college education has ended now that tuition has been imposed. Other programs are ending too; one program, sponsored by the city colleges at neighboring precincts, offered to policemen courses in the humanities, in psychology (on authority and its excesses), and in sociology (the poor).

In a *New York Times* Op Ed piece in 1976, an Open Admissions student at City College, Peter J. Rondinone, wrote beautifully of what Open Admissions had meant to many students who had failed in education beforehand. He spoke for the obstacles it faced, the gains it brought, the brief era it was.

When I went to City College in 1972, my vocabulary was limited to a few choice phrases like "Move over rover and let Petey take over." I still "hung out" on a Bronx street corner with a group of guys who called themselves the Davidson Boys and sang songs like "Daddy-lo-lo." Everything we did could be summed up with the word "snap." That's a "snap." She's a "snap." He had a "snap."

God only knows how I graduated from high school. I never went to classes. I'd spend my time on the front steps of the building smoking grass with the dudes from the dean's squad. I was a public school kid. The classrooms were overcrowded and the teachers knew it, so they made these weird deals with me.

If I agreed to read a book and do an oral report they'd pass me. So I graduated with a "general" diploma and applied to City College. The riots of '69 made it possible for me with that diploma, regardless of my class average, to enter. Now that open admissions is all but eliminated, I realize how fortunate I was.

I took the placement exams while nodding on "barbituates." That made freshman year difficult. The administration made sure I was placed in all three remedial programs: math, writing and college study skills. I was shocked. I had always thought of myself as a bright dude. I was the only guy in the neighborhood who read books.

I realized I had a lot of catching up to do, so I gave up pills; I avoided people because they were time-consuming, and I wrote an essay a day as part of the extra assignments I requested from my professors. Those were painful days. Professors would tear up my papers the day before they were due and tell me to start over again—with a piece of advice—"Try to say what you really mean." Papers I spent weeks writing. Yes, those were painful days. . . .

It's not easy being an open-admissions student. I always felt vulnerable. I knew I lacked basic college skills. I was handicapped; I was a man reporting to work without his tools. One day, I feared, the college would grab me, test me and embarrass me. So I smiled when I didn't understand; and I never admitted that I didn't "know" something, but sometimes it showed and I paid the price.

But that is all behind me now. I am one of those few individuals who was given a chance during a unique period in the history of American education to get a college education and I did. Unfortunately, it's unlikely that history will repeat itself unless the students of the 70's begin to fight for open admissions like students of the 60's.

6 Writing from a Culture

Writing—especially creative writing—is all too often a way of "finding oneself." People fed up with their lives—with their jobs, their marriages, their world—seek redemption in writing. All too often that writing is narrowly autobiographical; it lies on a couch without a doctor to listen. For writing to be interesting, the self must find an external world. Whitman, in our national verse anthem, "Song of Myself," writing of his isolation in every other breath, races away from it into the arms of mankind. "I am the mate and companion of people, all just as immortal and fathomless as myself." Whitman, prophet of democracy, lover of the bride and the groom, strove to escape a loneliness that has haunted our history. Out of myth and alienation, we have come to think of the writer as a rebel—and have forgotten how essential the structure of the world is, even for a rebel. The individual's sense of self, replacing class or social status as a locus of importance, searched for and celebrated, needs the external world to exist. Our most popular highbrow novelist, Saul Bellow, puts his characters squarely in a world he has studied. Robert Frost created a world in which the self could speak. The need is no different for the beginning writer than it is for those who enroll in creative writing courses or write on the sly.

Back when Open Admissions began, when black pride was reaching for definition, I had a class of SEEK students whose powers of expression emanated from their culture. Partly because ethnic culture fades as opportunities widen, culture as a subject hasn't sustained a class since. But here, in a remedial writing class, it brought forth competence and took the students to a land where the self becomes substantial.

Many of these students were classified as disadvantaged, but they were not deprived of family security. Although there were many absentee fathers, there were grandparents, mothers, aunts, and cousins to knit the family together. The habits and manners that unite a group, that make families and clans, constitute the culture. They deliver sustenance with which one recovers strength in time of trouble; they make joy possible. Family and rituals are part of culture, and students still had both to write about—Sunday church services and Sunday dinners—institutions that brought an extended family together. Bible-bred and family-oriented, they were in a way the last nineteenth-century Americans. Where urban life now frayed their culture, they were still close enough to it to mourn its passing. While young whites wrote best when rejecting the consumer culture around them, creating a culture of rejection, young blacks wrote in affirmation of a culture still practiced.

Their identity came in identifying their history. The best papers invariably described a town in the South they had grown up in or visited. "The Deserted Village," in America, is peopled still. The worst papers, the shortest, the most hollow, from blacks as well as whites, pitifully tried to describe the room in which the students lived. None has made himself king of that castle. Without a sense of place the self is a blank. It must either sit in a yoga position and contemplate infinity or get up and sing where others sing, whine where others whine.

Unfortunately the "self" is hardly a useful word any

longer. It has become a slogan, trivialized by various forms of "sensitivity training." Even as it has been adopted in schools it is a puny thing. For women in search of their identity there are the now-popular women's courses, where Erica Jong is read but the notable achievements of such women in American life as Eleanor Roosevelt and Frances Perkins are ignored; where such triumphs as Louise Bogan's collected letters, *What the Woman Lived,* the work of Emily Dickinson or of Margaret Fuller, are unknown.

When Emerson discovered American introspection and wrote in his *Journal* the rule of the modern mind, "Life consists in what man is thinking of all day," he alluded to identity through digestion of the world. The quest for "self" is, at its most tragic, the quest of a people who have lost identity.

The loss of coherent rituals that regularly connect people diminishes the possibilities of self-expression. As opportunities for social mobility, as ambitions are better realized, cultural connections are disrupted. Possessions replace shared tasks. Since it is out of one's identity that one writes, the loss of culture is one of the dark causes of the writing crisis.

Whitman sought meaning in Man and Nature. "I am he that walks with the tender and growing night;/ I call to the earth and sea half-held by the night . . ." Thoreau, a stylist of the first order, was not the misanthrope some critics make him out to be. While he cultivated solitude, he made of it the great American spiritual adventure. Visitors were welcome in the cabin at Walden; he returned to Concord and the family pencil business because he had "other lives to lead." While he railed against conventional work, he was at work all the time as an observer of nature—an ambassador to it— reporting back tirelessly in a highly wrought style. Like the journalist Mencken poking fun at convention a century later, he could get away with any outrage because of his style. His prickly attitude toward his fellow man was the price he paid for his art; he used their society to soar above. In nature he found his metaphor and gave us such American imagery as "The bluebird carries the sky on his back," and such admonitions for cultivating our own ground as "I never knew so much was going on in Smith's meadow."

The importance attached in this country to a literal self mistakes biography for art. Unflattering biographical facts threaten to sink the work—which is more noble always than the life. Americans would do well to learn and appreciate the wise words of Hawthorne, spoken by the poet in his story "The Great Stone Face": ". . . my life . . . has not corresponded with my thought. I had grand dreams, but they have been only dreams, because I have lived—and that, too, by my own choice—among poor and mean realities. Sometimes even—shall I dare to say it?—I have lacked faith in the grandeur, the beauty, and the goodness, which my own works are said to have made more evident in nature and in human life." Without metaphor to enlarge the self, without society to engage it, the self is as small as the biographical fault.

My SEEK students also found meaning in the order and habits of daily life. They lived in poor and mean realities, but they, too, went beyond, to culture, to Nature itself.

The class met in the afternoons in the flimsy interior of a synthetic red schoolhouse, one of York's temporary buildings before its move to a permanent location in Jamaica. Our ceiling rose to a gable above papier-mâché beams, the carpet was footprinted and littered—the room never had a wastebasket, and whenever I opened the desk drawer, looking for chalk, I found cigarette butts and crumpled containers. Still, the thistles of language grew.

Some students in the class were better than their placement tests had indicated. For James, who had already taken English 100, the class was a repeat. Out of the fourteen students, nine finished and passed. A few students simply couldn't bring themselves to write. They disappeared. One boy who dropped out was a victim of all the wrong reasons for going to college. He was there only because his father threatened to throw him out of the house unless he enrolled. The boy had had a job as a messenger at Tiffany's, liked it, and wanted to work his way up to the position of "runner." He took care of himself by misspelling outrageously— "pepal" for people, "moor" for more. In one paper he was trying to extol the virtues of a college education, but he didn't believe it and naturally misspelled the words.

In the values of some students the Protestant ethic accompanied the new black consciousness. One student, Leonard Rice, was an heir to the serious students of my generation of the thirties and forties. Tall, thin, and studious-looking, he bent over his work with a frown, yet he smiled easily. He was a grind with a grin. Usually wearing coat and tie, he always carried an attaché case packed with books and papers which he straightened whenever he removed anything; but he often came into class late. Leonard had gone to a community agency's Urban Skills Center before college and had gotten a good start. He came from a home of order and striving, as one paper of his revealed. Because we had just had a big snowfall and traffic snarl, I asked the students to write about how they had felt coming to school that morning in the storm. He wrote with the deliberate steps of a pilgrim.

The thought of having to tramp through the snow in boots made me go back to bed. I decided I would not go to school today. My teachers would understand and maybe they themselves would be absent. . . . At that moment my mother came in and asked me whether I was going to school or not. I told her I would not. It would depend on how bad the weather was. She said the chief problem was with the wind, not necessarily with the snow. It was only expected to accumulate about three to four inches. On hearing this I decided that I would try to make it to school. After all I have an obligation to myself to try and get as much education as possible. I remember what my uncle told me before entering college. When you enter college, you are considered an adult. You are expected to fulfill your obligations without excuse. Do not let rain or snow stop you from getting to school. A little snow or rain in the past has never injured anybody. Set a goal for yourself and stick to it.

In his writing was the sound of earnestness. The Postal Service—through "snow or rain"—could not be more reliable than he. His resolution was all the more remarkable for the anxiety that, coming over him, sometimes caused him to stutter. Terribly serious about his work, he seemed surprised that I thought his writing competent and interesting. In his final exam, he wrote a passage about gaining black pride. The exam question began with a passage from W. E. B. Du Bois in *The Souls of Black Folk:* "Here we have brought out three gifts and mingled them with yours: a gift of story and song —soft, stirring melody in an ill-harmonized and unmelodious land; the gift of sweat and brawn to beat back the wilderness, conquer the soil, and lay bare the foundations of this vast economic empire. . . . Nor has our gift of the spirit been merely passive. Actively we have woven ourselves into the very warp and woof of this nation—we fought their battles, shared their sorrow, mingled our blood with theirs, and generation after generation pleaded with a headstrong, careless people to despise not Justice, Mercy, and Truth, lest the nation be smitten with a curse." The question asked, "What do you think are the gifts of black culture that add to the meaning of life? What can the country as a whole learn from them? Have any of these, in your opinion, influenced American life?" Leonard Rice told of how he had discovered black music and how it called him away from black shame.

When listening to songs of old I can hear the sorrow and suffering of my people. The work songs are an example. They hit deep into my soul everytime I hear them. They bring out the suffering which black people of the past had to bear in order to stay alive.

The Gospel spirituals are another example of black music which is dear to me. In this type of music I see hope, the stimulus which helped to carry the black race through times of difficulty and depression. Many times I have heard people say that if it was not for the sweet melody of the Gospel songs they would have given up hope of surviving in America. When I first heard this I did not understand what was meant, but as I listened carefully, the message was soon driven into my heart.

After a intensive study into Gospel music I was driven into another type of music, which in my opinion has brought happiness into all souls black and white. This music is soul music. . . . Soul singers such as James Brown and Aretha Franklyn are shouting because they are delivering a message to the world. Their shouts are meant for expressing themselves. They are taking the soul out of Gospel music and using it in the songs they sing. The movement of their bodies as they sing is the movement of our ancestors in Africa. I am still studying soul music because I find that there is no limit to where it can go. For instance it has reached into the souls of white folks so much that white groups as the Osmond Brothers are now copying the style. This shows the impact of soul music on the American way of life. The Osmond Bros. record sales has increased tremendously since they dived into soul singing. I am glad because they do have soul. . . .

Jazz was created by black men. It was not until recently that I found this to be true. St. Louis Jazz for instance was the beginning point for Black Jazz musicians. Sure stars as Mr. Louis Armstrong started out by playing St. Louis Jazz and old rag time jazz. He also helped to shape jazz to the form it is today. In Louis Armstrong's playing you can see the smiling faces of Black men of the south when they were mistreated by whites. By this I mean they turned the other cheek. Jazz shows the gradual growing of the black race in America. All the events that took place in society reoccurred in Jazz music. Jazz music was the secret news carrier of the Black caucus. . . .

The Puerto Ricans are more African than many black people think. In their music they use the conga and bongo drums. They have been using it for years. They always looked to Africa for new ideas. In listening to their music the beat of Africa can be heard very clearly, so clearly that when they play at a night club no one can keep their seat. The Latin Musicians have taken pride in the black culture for most of their existence. This came as a shock to me. In my tender

years I always shunned anything African. When I saw that
a race which could pass for white, and in many instances do,
I finally realized what a fool I was. But when I look at it in
a time context I realized that I was young and did not know
better.

That essay was a pilgrimage, from shunning ethnicity to
hearing it in the heart. He had been caught by, and perhaps
he was overcoming, the terrible struggle Du Bois describes
in his book. "One ever feels his twoness,—an American, a
Negro; two souls, two thoughts, two unreconciled strivings;
two warring ideals in one dark body, whose dogged strength
alone keeps it from being torn asunder." Perhaps we are
approaching in this country Du Bois's then undisillusioned
goal: "this longing to attain self-conscious manhood, to
merge his double self into a better and truer self. In this
merger he wishes neither of the other selves to be lost. He
would not Africanize America, for America has too much to
teach the world and Africa. He would not bleach his Negro
soul in a flood of white Americanism, for he knows that
Negro blood has a message for the world. He simply wishes
to make it possible for a man to be both a Negro and an
American, without being cursed and spit upon by his fellows,
without having the doors of opportunity closed roughly in
his face." I like to think, in that class, we were moving an
inch in that direction.

Some other contemporary answers, although less sophisticated, are worth hearing. One boy, who had shown a grasp
of standard English in his class assignments, but slipped up
on the final exam, wrote:

> When black people first came to this country, our culture was
> taken away from us. With the help of blacks like W. E. B. Du
> Bois and many other black men and women, black people
> have begun to find their souls—who black people are, and
> what their souls are all about. Black culture has brought
> many gifts to the World, and the bigot country of America.
> . . . America wouldn't have music if it wasn't for black folks.
> For generations blacks shared their blood on the battle fields

dieing for this country, helping the country grow. White people who run the country now, and who will always run the country till they are voted down. They have try to conquer and control the way black people think as long as we been here. Black culture needs to be taught in schools, when blacks are young they need hero, black people must be taught about their people their history. Because when one has knowledge of himself or his people or family, one begins to love himself and his people. He begin to respect whats his and most of all respect others. . . .

The sublimity of those last lines goes beyond grammar. This student suffered a speech impediment that made him tremble, and made the words get stuck in his throat. But he was a good listener. Leaning back in his chair, he would stretch out, and hearing something he liked, his shy smile would break into laughter. In mirth and innocence, he was a Billy Budd. His writing contained many problems at the beginning of the course, but it was always marked by imagination. Gradually it improved to a workmanlike competence. One day, when for a writing assignment I put on the board three phrases for students to choose from, each phrase describing a different person, he chose "a boy nodding on a stoop," and wrote that "he would soon come falling down from his throne." In an autobiographical paper, he launched into his favorite childhood activity—keeping pigeons in his back yard.

I was really surprised at what I saw in pigeons. They were people to me, each of them belonging to their own family's of pigeons. The birds at the pet shop were extremely supreme to the birds who live in the street. The pigeons in the pet shops were properly fed and taken care of from generation to generation and it showed in their breed. The pigeons in the street were called rats because they ate almost anything in the street. . . . My father never understood what a pigeon coop was. He would beat me whenever I went there. He thought all birds were street birds with germs.

When one glimpses what people have endured, one knows their courage. Black novelists, like Richard Wright in *Black Boy,* have shown that racism, creating feelings of worthlessness, can come home in mistreatment of one's own. Racism may have come home, to this student, in a family-inflicted stammer. Against such wounds stands the strength of a culture. Perhaps it was his connections with culture that allowed him to smile.

Another boy, short, wiry, hiding in the back row but hearing everything, wrote in the exam his clear views on black achievements.

> I think just being Black is Beautiful. I think this country as a whole can learn a lot from us blacks. I do not think this country can go on without blacks. Whitey may not notice, but Blacky is getting involved. Blacky is taking his step in the world. We have more Black politicians, more Black sportsplayers, Blacks are starting to dominate sports. And when it comes to Soul music, Blacky puts it all together. . . . Even though we have struggled a lot in life, I am proud to be black. There will come a time when we can sit back and tell whites what to do. I'm not prejudice but there are a few whites who spoil the bunch. Not all whites hate Negros. Whites who like Blacks think they are very nice. Blacks are a lot of fun except when they are full of buss [whiskey]. So the only thing I myself can tell my Black Brothers and Sisters is to keep the faith. God do not like a person who hates so just keep on keeping on.

One day in class he had reported that whenever he "handed money in the hand" to a clerk in a supermarket, the clerk returned the change on the counter. "That burns me up," he said. Others in the class reported having the same experience—money returned on the counter as if the hand were untouchable. I also took the repeated incident as a racist act and expressed some outrage. That night when I told my wife, she said the same thing often happened to her. When the clerk didn't give her change back in her hand, she told me she had wondered, "Is it because I'm Jewish?" She had been able to laugh at herself and dismiss the notion. But a black person may never know. Because of his skin color he will be vulnerable to racism that often cannot be confirmed or denied.

The exam on black achievements brought a bristling reply from a husky girl. At first I thought she was shy because of the peculiar way she sat in her seat, sideways, never facing me. She sat there with her overcoat on for the two-hour period. "People still have the nerve," she wrote, "to ask, 'Have any of these gifts influenced American life?' Of course not. Not when we make up over 75 percent of the poverty and welfare list." Culture, alas, had eluded her, failed to bestow its grace. Sometimes I'd beseech her to turn front-ward in that seat, and she'd slide a little ways with a smile part sly and part pleased. One day at the beginning of the class I commented on there being no men there. I didn't know what a Pandora's Box that subject was for her. She grumbled, "We're better off without them," and then led her sisters into a denunciation of men, which she topped with the statement, "Men aren't worth much anyway." Matriarchy not only yields strength, but sometimes bitterness as well. "What's she getting in your class?" a young man I had taught the term before asked me in her presence. "She gives all of us an X. Give her an X too." Matriarch or not, she was still a person, with a special way of curling her lips in disgust. When the time came to fill out the teacher evaluation form, she wrote on her sealed envelope, which I was to turn in, "to be opened by authorize personnel only." I reminded her to put on the d.

Another student, a gifted but insecure young black man, wrote a hymn to the family, a part of culture he maintains that many people, both black and white, have lost. His writing depicts his family—or perhaps an idealized one—and suggests black family stability.

Consider the component parts that make up most families. The father, performing as the bread winner and creating the well known father image. The mother, caring, concerned and

loving as only a woman can. In general enhancing the love
and affection of the father. Children, be they boy or girl for
many families, are the reason for the ambition, initiative, love,
understanding that make life bearable. The family doctor, this
is or should be a member of the family. The family doctor is
the one who calls the various members of the family out of
sickness, into health. One exception is a case where a family
doctor had a patient for many years. He is well acquainted
with the medical history of this friend and patient. There were
times this patient visited him for regular check-ups, and always pleasantries were exchanged. But there came a time
when the patient reached a ripe old age of 82 and was weak
and underweight, was bothered with a stomach disorder,
could not walk because of weakness. A call was placed to this
family doctor, the situation explained, and this friend and
doctor of many long years answered by saying, "I do not
make housecalls."

One writing assignment was prompted by a piece we had
read by Arna Bontempts, "Why I Returned." Born in Loui-
siana, Bontempts came to prominence as a writer in Harlem
in the 1920s; later he chose to return to the South—in the
1950s—once the walls of segregation began to fall. In food
and shelter, in church and song, in work and games, in the
look of the sky and the land, southern culture held him. Of
the South my students wrote movingly. A girl of great sensitivity made Christmas on a lane somewhere in Florida come
back in a dream, not only of her growing up, but also of
human community. Days of cooking preceded nights of
neighbors enjoying each other's specialties; families visited
back and forth through Christmas week; in the communion
of eating there was hilarity and friendship. When she was
eleven, the girl had been sent for the summer to visit a
grandmother in Queens. She found out in September that she
was the only one who had thought she was going back home.
She had been in Queens ever since. Not surprisingly, she
hated her grandmother. In spite of this trauma, her face was
delicate and soft, like her writing. A nineteen-year-old

unwed mother, she came to class one day with her two-year-old child—as if to say she couldn't get a baby-sitter any longer. Though she had liked the class she never came back after that.

The class mourned the loss of culture to the North, to urban mobility, to modern times. For a stylish girl who played cards more often than she attended class, the culture of family and food, of custom and talk, had not been replaced —as it had been for others—by a growing interest in music or books. Beneath her blue-shadowed eyelids she had seen a lot she didn't like.

> Times are changing and so are people. In my younger days Sunday was the main day of the week for the family to get together and talk about the events that occurred during the week. On Sunday mornings I would wake up by the smell of pancakes. I could then get up and get ready for church. The whole family would be there and after church was over, we would then meet at someone's house to have dinner. I'm not saying that this was every Sunday, but when the family got together on Sunday. It seemed like Thanksgiving came more than once a year. But now Sundays are not what they used to be. Certain people in the family do not want to be bothered. And it seems that everybody wants to sleep late on Sunday morning after partying Saturday night.

From the discerning eyes in this class, a sense of loss burst forth like weeds in a vacant lot; the most moving paper, though not directly on custom, described an imaginary person, an old lady, living alone. The writer, a thin, determined girl, was desperately trying to break through in her writing. The words usually came out in the wrong order, with the wrong spelling, and in incomplete sentences. But often in the midst of all this was a lyrical line. One of her early papers, about a park glen, described "a butterfly touching down on a rock." She could work only from gentleness and didn't trust her gentleness enough. Her final paper, "The Time to Remember," on which she worked hard, is something of a masterpiece.

She sits in an old gray rocking chair in front of an old white country house. There she sits day in and day out, rocking forward and backward in that old chair. Her hair was a dark gray, her skin was as soft as cotton. The old woman sits there waiting for death, while the warm sun bathes her old body. She sits there dreaming of the old times when her children and grandchildren came to visit her. No one comes now, to visit the old woman, no one but a lonely little dog who wishes for someone to feed him. Once fed he too does not stay to keep the old woman company.

Sunday is the day the old woman waited for, because that is the day she puts on her old flowered dress and hat and walks down the road to the church. The church was a place where the old woman felt happy and alive, and could tap her feet to the music or even join the small children and sing along. From 9 A.M. to 9 P.M. the old woman's life was fruitful and alive, but when 10 P.M. comes the old woman starts the long walk back home to a cold and lonely house. Sunday is gone and Monday will come, bringing the hardships of before, pulling the old woman back to her old rocking chair to dream of the days of long ago and the night before.

The "old white country house," the "old gray rocking chair," the porch, and the church were the artifacts of culture left behind in the South. Culture—the ordinary rituals that give meaning to life—connects people to each other. Loneliness goes far back in our history and recurs as we are torn from our roots in the nuclear family by mammoth cities, and sprawling, characterless suburbia. We will find our identity not only in form, as Thoreau did in nature, but also with one another. And when we don't have a larger identity than ourselves—in family, in fellowship, in community, in some kind of group—we yearn for it in spite of our protestations about individuality. "Men work together . . . / whether they work together or apart," wrote Robert Frost in "The Tuft of Flowers." We need not merely lament the vacuum that the decline of cultures creates, but we can create the link, as Whitman and Frost did, with the missing others. The act of writing is an attempt to create what the world has denied or taken away. It is saying what one has never been able to say to another other human being. Poet that she was, Emily Dickinson used her loneliness to write: "This is my letter to the world/ That never wrote to me. . . . ."

In this land of change, where each generation has sought to create life afresh, nostalgia runs a close race with independence. In my family, customs that my parents had come to think tiresome, to me still assume a strange appeal. When growing up both my parents had sat at countless stuffy Sunday family dinners; as adults with children of their own, they dropped such convocations in favor of free Sunday activities they couldn't engage in during the week—gardening, sailing, reading. On a family visit to Memphis in the mid-sixties, I finally got a taste of a Sunday dinner with all the relatives sitting around, and recognized a common bond. We northerners all commented on how sad it was we didn't do that more often. We were all nostalgic for a ritual that, if practiced, probably would lose its appeal. Still, I long for Sunday dinners I never had—a Thanksgiving, as the student said, every Sunday.

The women in the class were quicker in noting modern losses, but the men were holding on tighter to their cultural heritage. Their white contemporaries, in their agrarian work clothes, were searching for an identity the young blacks could already lay their hands on. And in black history, in recognition of music as well as bravery, they were finding the identity black women had long found on the porch. A student in the class all too briefly, and one of the most articulate students I have had, brought much of the new thinking together. He saw that the hideous South had a touch of the sublime. What Arna Bontemps had pointed to in the essay, what is becoming apparent, he sensed: The South may now offer a more fulfilling life to black Americans than the North that many have fled to. Not only is there land and less crowding, but between blacks and whites in the South there is a common culture, a way of perceiving life, a common tongue. Blacks and whites in the North don't have a culture to share, to help them "get over"; but now that the burning crosses are doused, the common culture moves the South forward. About the power of that culture I know something from both my mother, who overcame her prejudices but kept her culture in the North, and a little from my cousins in the South. My mother's father was noted for having hidden in his house blacks hunted by lynch mobs. And as fiery a gentleman as Du Bois noted that all was not hate between white and black in the South, but that in relationships that were fundamentally wrong there could be a trust acted on, a sympathy transmitted.

Talking in class about the Bontemps piece, Richard Lester gave us this news. "Where I went to school in South Carolina the school is now successfully integrated. Whites are showing a new respect for blacks. Even when they weren't you knew where you stood and you had a culture. I went to a segregated school and was taught black history. Sure, they only taught us about George Washington Carver. But you have to see these people in historical perspective. One of the spokes of the wheel is Malcolm, another is Martin Luther King. But they are all turning in the same identical direction." Lester pinned culture down to the specific and saw a specific influence on whites. "It's in food. Whites now eat black food. It's in the gospel songs. And whites in the South sing our gospel songs."

I could hear in his voice the careful pitch of thinking and the pauses of deliberate choice. A light, slim, muscular twenty-seven-year-old, with a well-defined face, he was taking a crack at college. He had apparently risen through the ranks of a local antipoverty agency. How the testing devices ever placed him in the basic remedial course I'll never know. In his writing, spirit and mind, the old and the new, spoke together. His paper on an experience that had meant something read as follows:

> We arrived in Pine Hill, New York, one Saturday morning around nine o'clock, after leaving New York City at daybreak. The trip out of New York City was at best mediocre,

with the exception of the usual excitement on leaving the city. When we arrived the sun was hot, but instead of being uncomfortable it only amplified the beauty of the countryside and made it all the more brilliant. The air was clean, sweet and made one glad to be alive. The trees stood as though they were planted by nature in a perfect pattern. You could almost hear them speak in some strange language of beauty and majesty. The large trees stood over the small trees as a mother stands over a child; protecting them, teaching them, giving them an example of what to be.

As we walked along the trail on the side of the mountain it became obvious that man with his technology and knowledge was a very minute thing, incapable of creating with a great deal of effort what nature can create effortlessly. The mountains were sublime in their timeless effort to make a home for the living things of the forest. Looking out over the sun-drenched, round, smooth, green mountains, one could, regardless of religious beliefs, see God. The giant green God of Nature. The God that tirelessly changes, but never changes.

You think, you think of birds, rabbits, insects, bears, flowers, grass and even snakes. You think of life, of freedom, of death. You think of how they live together with only survival to think of and react to. You think of man, you think of men. You think of the unnatural world that man has made. You think of the unnatural deeds that men have done. The feeling of being in a world of unreality comes over you until you realize that this is the world of reality and the world of man is that of unreality. As you turn to walk down the trail you look back at the mountain untouched by man, and unconsciously say a prayer that it stays that way.

When we returned to dinner everyone was quiet, quiet with a sense of contentment that can only be attained through a feeling of complete freedom. After dinner everyone went out by the lake to watch the sun go down. The lake seemed to fall asleep as the sun went down and you got a feeling of security just watching it, for you knew that the sun would come up again if only to awaken the lake.

Night fell and the creatures of the night started to sing the timeless song of love, the song of mating. The sky is clear and the stars are out. You wonder about the distance the light had to travel. It seems the light traveled trillions of miles, millions of years just for you. The mountains are gone now, devoured by the night. So you retire also, for you too have become a part of nature.

You are awakened the next morning by the sound of rain. You look out the window to see the rain coming off the trees. At first you are disappointed because you can't go out, but then you think that this is nature's way of keeping her mountains full of the life that she so diligently watches over. So you sigh and discard your feeling of selfishness.

It finally stops raining but it's time to return to the city. As you prepare for the return trip, you are surrounded with sadness for having to leave, but glad that you were able to, if only for a short while, be a part of the beauty of nature. As you go down the winding road you look out at the gray cloud moving slowly over the mountains as if checking to be sure its job was well done. You leave, but you take part of the country with you, and you leave part of yourself with the country.

Nature won out over technology, its victory celebrated by an able writer (even if he did let an advertising jingle influence that last line). I don't know what happened to this student. After turning in two long, splendid papers he stopped coming to class. His counselor, without giving any reason, said he had withdrawn.

Many in the class were older students who were returning to college. Of these, women are often exemplary students. An attractive, well-dressed lady in her late twenties, with children at home, was briskly going about getting an education. She had already passed Freshman Composition, with a *B*, but insisted on taking this basic remedial course because she wanted to work on her writing. She was a bit impatient with the past. She found Du Bois old-fashioned and to his litany of "story, song, and spirit" replied in class one day, "We've

had enough of singing." But without black music, America
would be as musical as Iceland. Many of Du Bois' passages
stirred the others, but she kept refuting them. One line of his
she didn't get at all: "Would America have been America
without her Negro people?" The *her*, she found, implied
ownership. The compact, made out of song and sweat, didn't
get through—*her* because blacks had given so much. Mrs.
Howard was a considerable stylist in her own right, as in this
description of New York.

Park Avenue, from forty-second to ninety-eighth Street, is
an area of cleanliness and whiteness. The streets are fresh and
warm; the atmosphere light and gay. Tall buildings stretching
to all heights give one the feeling of power, greatness and
unlimited possibilities. One can climb, know no bounds and
realize all potential; there is order, freshness and cleanliness
here. I continue uptown, my spirits are high. Maybe I can
accomplish, maybe I can succeed. Everything is orderly, no
garbage in sight, the shops bustle with activity. Trees are
everywhere and each street bursts with variety. Each offers
novelty and excitement.

Ninety-sixth Street is a wide boulevard or dividing line.
The island of trees in the middle of the avenue ceases to exist.
An overhead el sharply comes into view. The gust of cold
wind, caused by the speeding train, hurtles cutting bits of
filthy reality into my face and into my eyes. Before me long
streets are lined with distorted garbage cans, their lids flat-
tened, hopelessly trying to contain their contents. Those less
successful abundantly spill their innards onto the street. Others, tired of standing up against a losing battle, topple over in
defeat. The trees are gone and two colors remain—black and
gray. Every street is different, each more filthy than the other.
Shadows, alleys and tunnels are everywhere, reeking with the
acrid odor of human waste. The buildings appear stunted and
others though tall are the same. There's no individuality, no
expression, no challenge, no flexibility, and no promise. They
are rigid, rigid, and seem to say these streets will not change,
conditions will not change and you shall not change.

Read aloud, her papers were instructive. Once, when I asked her how she had gone about writing a paper, she summed up a lot of my advice admirably, for everybody's benefit. "I get everything out and then go back and clean up the mess." When I despaired of helping a slim, wavering girl, whose writing was chaotic, I asked Mrs. Howard to go over a paper with her. And the paper, gruesome as it was, became grammatical. It was about a two-hundred-pound woman who beat her dark-skinned children, plunged them into a hot bath, and rubbed their backs with salt.

It was a varied class. In it, James had "gotten over." Two fine students—a man and woman—had left, along with a reluctant youngster. A matriarch had adjusted a bit in her chair. Two girls skimpy on attendance had managed to write passing exams and complete their work. From the stammers of a boy beaten in childhood and the hand of a girl paralyzed with determination, much beauty had come. Mrs. Howard and Leonard Rice had done serious, thoughtful work. The slim, faltering girl had coughed to the point of my running, finally, for a glass of water, afraid she would choke; she had learned something and, wisely, transferred to a community college's nursing program. In our cluttered room the students' writing had responded to prodding, to my going over their work with them; we had found common ground. Toward the end of the term we had read Langston Hughes' tale "Cracker Prayer," and the juices of irony in a white southerner praying had pleased them. "Lord, Lord, dear Lord, since I did not have a nice old colored mammy in my childhood, give me one in heaven, Lord. My family were too poor to afford a black mammy for any of my father's eight children. I were mammyless as a child. Give me a mammy in heaven, Lord. . . . But, Lord, if there be educated Nigras in heaven, keep them out of my sight. The only thing I hate worse than an educated Nigra is an integrated one. . . ." Something fundamental had gone well in that class, for I got away with a satire on my own role. When I suggested that they must now spot their own errors in their essays, that I wasn't going to sit next to them anymore, the wordplay was irresistible. "Your cracker pappy isn't always going to be at your side." They laughed. It was a nice class. We had become black and white people again.

7 Happy Writers

Hello, Doc. Funny me being in this predicament again. Oh yeah!, Doc I've read plenty of books on identity with first accordance to myself. In other words Doc, I'm trying to relate. There was an old saying, and there still is, that every man and women has a psychological problem of their own, and I do too, but that's not the problem. My identity is, and I don't mean the kind where Uncle Sam knows that I still exist on the face of the earth. For I one day will have a little Brick house with a garage and basement, with a 30 by 40 foot lawn with green grass, and a maple tree, with a german shepard and an Kitty Kat constantly running around it. I guess in some instances this can be considered a new era of a black man's dreams of living in America, in relationship to his well being. I know that I have to be a good social security no. to pursue these goals.

Doc, of course, was the instructor, me. The student, Ronald, was speaking on the handwritten page, speaking his way into literature. The paper was entitled "I thank you" and was 1500 words of clear and dense philosophy spinning off Eldridge Cleaver's *Soul on Ice* and landing upright on its own ground. The class was the third in the remedial sequence

—dealing with literature and ideas—and it was the first one in which I had met an aspiring Plato. About the self he was always original. A serene presence, a tall young man in a T-shirt, a face of polished black, the nose of a Roman and the eyes of a searchlight—these were all Ronald's. Often he wore a white sailor's hat, brim turned down, over his noble head. One day when we were talking about Thoreau's view of a house—beautiful if it was unadorned wood and windows —he looked up, his eyes a pool of light, and said he wanted a sliding glass door looking out on a green lawn. Under the title "Thoreau's Power," he wrote:

> A baby cries forever, the housing developments stretch to the gateways of heaven, Satan puts on a Santa Claus suit and sells time by the hour. The Revolution will not be televised on TV. Thoreau presents these reality-stricken episodes in technicolor. Thoreau doesn't say what these reality-stricken episodes are, because he speaks of nature. [He didn't bother to say what they are either.] Through his highly-strung lust for nature's existence, he makes you think about problems from A to Z, and not just in a black and white image.
>
> Imagine if you could kill time without injuring eternity. If you can remember back a month ago, what you did to your clocks and watches, you'll begin to see man's mockery of time.

He paraphrased Thoreau and brought in daylight saving as an example. "Powerful steps of nature march into your very uncanny non-knowing illiteracy. For all we know the problems of the world are factors of time. Time is mankind's unsolved problem."

He would be welcome, along with poets and woodchoppers, in Thoreau's bare cabin. "The real thoughts and actual actions of Thoreau's writing on Nature aren't just to be read or written about, but dreamt about for 1000 days times a hundred. They aren't just to be kept in America, but to be handed over to German schools, Russian schools, and not studied upon, but relinquished like the world's last cup of water. This is the power and glory of Thoreau's effect upon man in dealing with nature, truly a gift from nature."

At first Ronald's writing was murky with occasional drops of clear imagery. What could I say but "What do you mean; say it clearly; don't leave us wondering"? I gave him the punctuation exercise and he came back with a fresh draft. And the thoughts and images from his lens on eternity gained clarity and correctness. "Ralph Ellison's Invisible Man has no name. No name, therefore no social security number. With passing thoughts of days, yesteryears, and important decades, he rides his small white donkey and still reminds us that we have a time limit to fulfill and not just to be alive to be alive. Things begin to happen to Ralph Ellison's Invisible Man at accutron pace. . . ."

I had urged him to give that small white donkey his head, to see what the donkey represented. So Ronald continued, "And as we begin to see the small white donkey trots forward onto the sky's limit, and even onward. For now we begin to see the white donkey as a time piece in relationship to his rider, the Invisible Man. . . . The relationship between inner reckoning is a national universal thing that happens to all black people in some sense or form of happening. The white donkey represents this image of time in true reality. . . ." Ah, poet-philosopher, time and infinity are forever your concerns; and I, the teacher, follow you with awe, the fly at the donkey's rear. How hard it was—when you thought so deeply, when in between clarities you fell into clouds—to confess that I didn't always understand; how hard when you wrote with such imagination to remind you that clarity, even spelling, could do honor to your thought. Unlike many poets and philosophers, you stoically bore the wounds of criticism and healed them.

While some black students found *Soul on Ice* impenetrable, Ronald had no trouble with it. I don't think I'll teach *Soul on Ice* in a black class again. The sexual confusions that Cleaver sorts out—his fantasy and literal rape of white women as an act of revenge—are too much for many to bear. While the girls said about his final hymn of love to the black woman, "It's about time," many of the young men couldn't react out of numbness. Ron went after the subject of identity, and in particular Cleaver's way of finding identity through the example of others—Malcolm X, Elijah Muhammed, and Chris Lovdjeff, the Christlike prison teacher. He knew that identity was a complicated business and, refusing to simplify it, raised important questions.

> In many cases it seems as if identity is an object that lies on the outside of a person. To secure this so-called outside thing, he must find out about himself on the inside. . . . He shows us . . . that it is something that must be searched for, and then grasped and secured, like the birth of a Mother's baby. . . . I can't say what identity is, for I'm searching for mine. But I say I admire him [Chris Lovdjeff] for something he has. . . . He teaches a criminal, a convict, the illiterates, and enjoys man's love of love itself. He treasures man's work. Above all he helps. Is it an identity that he identifies himself with? . . . Eldridge through Chris Lovdjeff presents identity as an outside thing, which isn't a force. The reason for that is that you must search and find it. I think we can now begin to realize it as a destination you reach within your life period.
>
> The inner thing of you fights, and tears down, and puts up, until the mind, soul and heart, as well as the physicalness of the body is satisfied by a catch of impostorship, until they which is you realized that the impostor was just a passing substitute almost like that of a Lust which dies after many vices of life, until the day of ultimate happiness comes. Sometimes I wonder if it will then last you forever. . . .

When I talked to the small class of eight students, Ronald would tilt back in his chair, show the profile of a black Cicero, and stroke his chin—critic and appraiser of verse. Pick up a thought of his, and he would turn with a grin, but not necessarily a comment. When it was all over, and we met on the street, he broke into a smile showing brilliant teeth, stretched out an arm, and said, "That was a lovely class."

He wrote an explosive exam. The fog that obscured his mind at the beginning had rolled out to sea. The grammar was strong at the start, he knew his subject so well. The first question was not written with him in mind, but he grinned when he saw it: "The quest for identity is never easy. To discover oneself, one must reject standards set by the world. *Soul on Ice, Walden,* and *The Invisible Man* are each concerned with the problem and move from rejection to affirmation. The journey brings out the definition. Write a coherent essay, using specifics from each book, to develop a definition of identity." Here is Ronald's essay:

Eldrige Cleaver, an immortal called Thoreau, along with a sidekick named Ralph Ellison present to us, ourselves living and wondering about the next 24 hours.

In the reward, called *Soul on Ice,* Cleaver sends me through time, without ever counting or knowing the number situation. The book, (excuse my wording) is so damn intensified about Cleaver's struggle, that the relationship between me and him, makes us seem as twin brothers. Already the world or the system of the United States *rejects* him. I guess you can argue with me that he rejects himself from the system, because he had to get to jail someway. From his rejection he gathers Knowledge from Knowledge givers, such as Chris Lovdjeff. In my Animated story of living well, I would say that Cleaver lives like a prince. For when is a prince happy but when he has everything he desires in mind as well as physical attainment.

Then so is Eldrige Cleaver, he begins to destroy the fact that men are institutionalized or stymied by the American ways of living. Cleavers developes his mind in jail, he begins to find who he's going to follow in the religious world. It so happens that he chooses Malcolm X. He begins to destroy his grandfather thoughts and even perhaps his son's thoughts if he is ever to have one, about that of white women.

He finally realizes that white women are commercial capital endeavors that the U.S. grants you not in love terms. The journey for Eldrige Cleaver I say is one that bestowed upon him like wood is to fire, with it's redness, and destroying touch. Identity, it frightens me, when I begin to see men destroy the wants of themselves and eat reality.

Eldrige eats and then lets it shine upon us through the identity sense. He makes us aware of ourselves in which we begin to check ourselves out.

"He ain't heavy, he's my brothers." I often don't take a likening to people in general period. It goes double for white people. I most honestly confess that I cling to and live by people as the late Robert F. Kennedy, Doc Wheeler, Yul Brenner, and Thoreau. These people posses goodness by the dollar times the minute. Now you can begin to see the rich-, ness in goodness almost like Coca Cola in goodness.

Thoreau takes us not on trips or wishes, he trusts us like we were his children. The thing that I cling to most in Thoreau is his quietness. It reminds me of the stars and planets painted in color, with a strict vividness on red, blue and black, and without any sound at all, again I say this is the quietness of this man. You Doctor Wheeler, and perhaps three million more would say that his identity is in nature. I send it through Congress that I tend to disagree. His identity is in that of men. He has examined mind and ways of men so long and so much that nature is escapism for him. With it's still water's of the marsh land, and chipperills laughing at me, and rabbits playing games with chipmunks, this is where he finds I confess his identity. This brings me to the question who am I to say what identity is? When you see the quietness in a man like that of the future called space, and nature laughing with him at you, you to can begin to see the identity of a immortal called Thoreau.

Rejection skims itself with Ralph Ellison. He takes life in stride, identity becomes a quest. Not a sidekick, after all. I would say in some instances the complete man. Identity prolongs itself here. His grandfather dies leaving a momentum, that he was a natural born traitor all his life. What did he mean to his grandson at that time, and does it still relate to himself now. Blacks rejects each other because of the state they are in. Ralph Ellison goes through changes in convincing us that he was an invisible man. He takes us from childhood to Delinquency of the mind. He shows us that it isn't easy. identity through these writers is a journey with yourself about yourself. He presides around those who come in contact with you. It hurts and is sometimes tiresome, but it's worthwhile. You know me, and yes is yes to you as well as dying for your rights and wishes, not identity in a longrun, but a beginning of me knowing.

Well, Doc, what do you do with the joy of Ron? What do you do with his American lingo imaginatively used—until it falls from fatigue into foggy verb forms, misspellings, false apostrophes. I send it through Congress that you are a man of original talent, a victim of "man's unsolved problem"—time itself. As you race headily through a two-hour exam, you pay the cost in losing a period after an hour and a half. A wrong word, like *likening,* has the absolutely right meaning. What do you do when you ride in the company of Yul Brynner? You go on eagerly to the next question, rather flatly put, Doc, by yourself: "Choose any two poems from Dickinson, Yeats, or Auden and show how the idea of the poem becomes effective through imagery and sound pattern."

Emily Dickinson
    Hope is the thing with Feathers
    It asked a crumb of me, sea's that I've never heard of. Imagine what color they are at the bottom. Land's colder the North and South Dakotas. Sores that are storm throughout the universe. Hope it is—thing with feathers. This all comes to the imagination of reading this poem. Again if hope is the thing with feathers, is there a god so almighty. Hope, sweetest, the thing, abash the little, chillest. Words that show through sound, sight. The words are good to the ear as well as mind. Producers of thought are there main inferences through Sound pattern.
    A bird came down the Walk. He did not know I saw, he drank. Imagery begin to destroy senses in the last stanza.

> Oars divide the Ocean
> Two silver for a Seam,
> Or butterflies, off banks of noon,
> Leap, plashless as they swim.

Question presented to me are what is water to do with the bird drinking of a dew. Effectiveness in words are velvet head with its tender touch, glanced with rapid eyes as if to be afraid of weary of something. Leap, plashless, as they swim. The relationship of fish and birds, seems to be the that of freedom. Is anything free at all, can it fly to mars the bird or even to California, without being soared down upon by a eagle like raindrops hitting a 5th Ave jewelry shop. Awareness of things are brought through Miss Emily Dickinson in life, nature, and present self.

Some teachers ask for a paraphrase of a poem and get one in prose. Who ever got a paraphrase that was a poem in itself? Ronald took the sounds, the words, and dropping them in and adding his images, created and re-created. To the very end, he would hold on to such stumblestones as "the that of freedom." He struck at essences, in a clear sentence: "The words are good to the ear as well as mind." He knew what poetry was. And he had raised important questions amid blazing images: "Is anything free at all . . . ?" He had lost his grip but shown his hold too. I've rarely seen an exam where the grip doesn't slacken, and have seen the grammar perfect where there was no passion.

An instructor must go through the agony of balancing content and expression. Ronald never would have written as imaginatively—and as clearly as he now did—if his thought hadn't been encouraged, his grammar nudged. Oh, I know teachers who would have flunked him on his first papers and right through—and muffled his voice altogether. I had never graded a paper of his until I could give it a *C* or better; and I had seen him rise into the *B*s. My first impulse after reading the exam was to give him an *A,* and to proclaim him a poet-philosopher to all who knew him. But, Doc, think of the effect on Ron. He would think he could write carefree, for the applause. We both needed reality. I gave him a *B plus* on the exam, a *B* for the term.

I'm glad I tempered my enthusiasm—and three years later, when standards tightened, probably would have tempered it more. Had Ronald been a student in 1977, there would have been a postremedial essay exam to take, which he probably would have failed. His previous teachers—and I too—should have insisted on more tutorial help. Yet bypassing relatively small errors was perhaps the cost of his gaining clarity, of bringing his inspiration to light—even if the errors would finally loom large.

A year and a half after this course, he did take another English course—an introduction to western literature from the Greeks to Dante, given by a traditional teacher. When the teacher showed me Ron's final paper, I was appalled; I, too, would have flunked him. But in the teacher's handwritten note at the bottom of the paper was criticism of the most destructive kind: "It's not me you can't write for," the professor had written. "You can't write the English language." Ron's writing *had* deteriorated and so the professor had risen to defend "standards," but apparently without conveying any respect for the student's mind. When I told him how promising a writer Ronald had been, the professor said, "You can't coddle them forever." He was right—the trouble was that Ronald hadn't been coddled long or steadily enough before meeting an acid test. Alas, he was the victim of time; he flunked out of college after three years.

Papers on literary topics only come alive when the student reacts to a book rather than when he lets the book itself write the paper. A good paper, I advise all students, is a meeting halfway or thereabouts between what the book tells him and what the student doesn't yet realize he knows; the book and the student must interact. Details from the book must not be ignored; they must be used once they have awakened his sleeping mind. A year later, in this same course, another SEEK student let *The Invisible Man* illuminate values he had never, perhaps, clearly stated before.

The identity seeking individual roams through a jungle of fruit and cannibals, his head twisted straight, his eyes pressed forward as he travels the light and dark paths to his success.

He is kept on the run in fear of man eaters that lurk behind trees. The invisible man was kept running by Bledsoe who used his college position to hide his true heritage. The individual runs across field after field looking for a path to his identity as did the invisible man who moved from job to job in search of himself. In pace with time the individual runs, passing those who make room for him to cut the way for all. The Mary's who insist that the individual become something that will be a credit to the race make room for him.

Sometimes the individual is caught in a narrow field and has to fight for his independence. The invisible man fought Brockway to obtain his individuality at Liberty Paints. In a large field the individual may be caught by a clan of blood thirsty witch doctors like the Brotherhood that'll promise to show him the way through the jungle. Even make him a leader. Give him a staff to lead his people and maybe throw in a chain from a rabbit's foot to bring him good luck. In this field the individual may meet oppositions that'll make him wonder which is witch.

If the individual is to find his own way through the jungle he must learn the many paths to success and travel downhill as well as up. It was possible for the invisible man to get kicked out of college and become a leader of Harlem. The individual must also acquire x-ray vision to see behind trees, through men and anticipate reactions. He must learn to take the shape of the container he's put in yet still retain his own mind.

Rather than scholarly, this paper is wise. And rather than using his education for scholarship, this student is using it for life. *Which is witch* has wit and *downhill as well as up* has the phrasing of the whole.

In the course prior to this, students are introduced to literary topics through a novel or play. I have often used Malamud's *The Assistant,* Wright's *Native Son,* Hemingway's *A Farewell to Arms,* and Lonne Elder's fine play, *Ceremonies in Dark Old Men.* Carson McCullers, Saul Bellow, and Nathaniel Hawthorne have also proved their worth in my class. In essays and exams, my students discuss problems raised by literature, letting the books sharpen and develop their observations of life. To relate literature to life is not only to do it justice, but also to allow the student to write beyond himself, about ideas.

"Life is unfair," said President John F. Kennedy. "Some are born rich and some are born poor. Some are born sick and some are born well." This remark of Kennedy's, made at a press conference when he was asked about the fairness of the draft, began the essay question in English 110. The students were to use *A Farewell to Arms, Ceremonies in Dark Old Men,* and their own observations of life to comment on overcoming unfairness. "Illusion," the question said, "can often be a way of survival, but too much illusion can destroy." One answer gave a beautiful, sad paraphrase of the Kennedy quote: "Some are born dim, dark and black with hate and malice, while others are being sprinkled white with brotherhood." Another reported directly from life, "Most of us have some kind of illusion that helps us to face our reality." In this class, composed mostly of blacks, a few Puerto Ricans, and two whites, nobody attacked the life force. "We have to work around it and live life with all the unfair things that help to create it." Perhaps the most astonishing piece came from Rafael, who didn't bother with the literature at all. A fast talker, he had a wife, child, and full-time job, and could have done nicely without the latter, which kept him away from class too often. "Life is not unfair," he announced, "it is beautiful. Nature has made us what we are and has given us a purpose to accomplish in life. It is unfortunate that some are born poor, others are born sick and some die young, but that is nature's way of balancing the structure of human society. . . . Nature controls every move we make in life. Whether we're rich or poor, well or sick and whether we live a long time or die young. We have all been programmed by nature to forefill a purpose in life and that purpose as far as I can see is to live life under any condition and enjoy the beauty of life for what it is. There is nothing more beautiful in this world than to be able to breath air and say, I'm alive! Have a nice summer."

Even students who baffled and irritated me during the term sometimes turned in a remarkable essay. A stringy black kid with the bounce of a basketball player in his walk, George had resisted doing all of the assigned classwork. He announced in class he would not read *A Farewell to Arms* because he had already read it in high school. Maybe he had read it, maybe he hadn't; in any case he was proud of not having to read it again. Before writing his essay on the subject of illusion, he asked me what illusion meant. I told him it was "something that exists in your head but not in reality" and was prepared for a juvenile exploration. George wrote:

Life is, as president John F. Kennedy said, unfair. Some are born rich and some are born poor. Some die young and some die old. As people grow out of the adolescent stage into young adulthood they suffer a certain amount of defeat. People must break, because no one is perfect, that is why they are still on earth. There are those who are close to being perfect. We call these people illusions.

Illusions do not remain in this world very long. Just long enough to complete the job that they were sent to do. Illusions may appear in all types of forms. But in the book *A Farewell to Arms* Henry's illusions appeared in the form of a woman. Her name was Catherine. When henry first met her she was a carefree person, who did not value the gift of love. Henry met Catherine during war time.

Catherine loved henry. She also knew what henry's weakness was. Catherine once had a weakness herself. She over came her weakness when the man who she loved died in the war. Catherine taught henry and he soon grew to love her and needed her. He was learning the value of life. Catherine's mission was completed. For doing such a good job with henry, Catherine was awarded the key to the gates of heaven. She knew she had to leave this world and did so giving birth to henry's child. Henry learnt well the values of life and now it was time to teach some one else. Comparing my self to henry I see a very close relationship. I too am a person who was given birth by my mother and place on earth to do gods work. God is also an illusion. He is a perfect illusion that we all love and respect. That is why he does not live on the planet earth.

I too may become an illusion one day. I will pass my knowledge on to others, and they will have followers behind them. For if we must die, let us not die a foolish man but a wise man who loves his people as he loves himself.

He had written not only out of observation but out of innocence as well (of capital letters too). And in his innocence, he had arrived at a sophistication only purity can achieve. When I went to college, answers like these—though decidedly different—were considered by students to be "throwing the bull"—and won good grades. George had searched and he had thought. His last line took off, unwittingly or not, from Claude MacKay's famous poem passed around at Attica, "If we must die, let us die like men not like hogs penned up. . . ." His little piece had many influences. He had been ingenious. An English professor, when I showed it to him, asked with amazement, "You think that's good?" He passed English 110, but not the literature course that followed it. Still, I agree with a nonacademic friend who said of this work, "It's beautiful." Innocence can produce wonders, but, in George, it didn't retain its force, or turn into knowledge.

Purity of mind and the brilliance of a single vision came forth from another student in a paper on Hawthorne's story "The Great Stone Face." Perhaps it was at the expense of leaving a few things out that this young man could write so clearly and originally. Only an athlete brought up in the black church could have written the first sentence; only an American tied to a culture could have entertained these ideas as sincerely and as well.

A myth, like competition, brings out the best in a man. A man that has a myth to honor has a purpose in life. He often succeeds in his aim. A myth is a beautiful attraction to the eyes of man.

In the story, "The Great Stone Face," Ernest had a myth to honor that was called the great stone face. The great stone face was a rock that resembled a human countenance.... The inspiration that this rock gave Ernest made him a very honest young man. He knew who he was and what he was living for. The great stone face not only inspired Ernest's life, but it gave him a deeper understanding of what peace, love, and understanding was all about. The great stone face also instilled goodness and kindness in Ernest. The great stone face also gave Ernest the true qualities of what it takes to be a man.

Having a myth to follow, Ernest was a very respectable child. Ernest was very obedient and respectful to his mother, because he knew that if he disrespected his mother, it would not make him faithful to his myth. He was dutiful to his mother, and helpful to her in many ways. He was always around when he was needed. He would feed the chickens, give water to the horses, and help his mother clean the house. Ernest grew up to be a fine young man.

In life, everyone should have a myth to honor. Having a myth to honor gives a person a sense of direction. Not only should everyone have a myth, but we should build it high, and name ourselves after it.

8 American Literature and Writing

A nation that doesn't recognize its own literature will never be civilized. English letters served and civilized us in our beginnings. Now that we have developed a literature addressed to our national situation, written in our idiom, we cannot afford to ignore it.

Thus, the teaching of American literature to teachers, the teaching of it in our schools, becomes the partner of a writing restoration. Young people still stagger across the moors of *Wuthering Heights* and experience trouble writing themselves, when they might see through the wilderness of Hawthorne or Conrad Richter and learn how to write their own history.

American literature has not only contained American idiom while keeping some quaint accents and old usages but also come forth in its most civilized voice with the pith of plainness. There is surely the baroque in our literature, but even Henry James, becoming more elaborate in his style the longer he lived away from America, the more he sought a sensuous home in his art, could, returning in 1903, write of a New England autumn in *The American Scene:* "There is a voice in the air, from week to week, a spiritual voice: 'Oh, the land's all right.'"

American prose and poetry is built of clear symmetry. Within its brevities, sound patterns and parallelism are distinctly American. Hear Emerson's indisputably American language: "Man is surprised to find that things near are no less beautiful and wondrous than things remote. The near explains the far." Or Thoreau, speaking of integrity: "Any truth is better than make believe. Tom Hyde, the tinker, standing on the gallows, was asked if he had anything to say. 'Tell the tailors,' said he, 'to remember to make a knot in their thread before they take the first stitch.' His companion's prayer is forgotten." Our first national words were in parallelism, "life, liberty, and the pursuit of happiness." In carving a life out of the chaos of Europe, out of waste and wilderness, in pushing away the overgrowth of one civilization and clearing the forest and vine for our own, we carved a language of lucidity. Of course we had textbooks too of the plainest English, the King James Bible, the other Elizabethans as well as American primers. Lincoln hewed the word: "that government of the people, by the people, for the people shall not perish from the earth." Lincoln also declared for grammarians to hear: "With educated people, I suppose, punctuation is a matter of rule; with me it's a matter of feeling. But I must say I have a great respect for the semicolon; it's a useful little chap." FDR was a native orator from the public platform: "The only thing we have to fear is fear itself." When Adlai Stevenson said in his 1952 acceptance speech, "There are no gains without pains," he was quoting from Benjamin Franklin's *Poor Richard's Almanac.*

In more fanciful poetry and prose, neither pith nor plainness is missing, the rails are split and polished, the language sits in a bold balance. "She was a rich mine of life, like the founders of early races," wrote Willa Cather in *My Antonia.* "The problem of the twentieth century is the problem of the color line," wrote W. E. B. Du Bois as the century began. The singular American balance shines in Robert Frost: "One luminary clock against the sky / Proclaimed the time was neither wrong nor right. / I have been one acquainted with the night." While Hemingway was not the first to pare the

American language down to strong and hard meaning, he was the most luminous practitioner of the American art of language whittling. "Isn't it pretty to think so?" says his maimed hero at the end of *The Sun Also Rises*, irony standing forth because of the plainness. Of novelists today, Saul Bellow mixes native idiom and the abstract. We need not honor only the complex, modern situation in American letters. In Whittier and Longfellow, we have native poets, neglected in schools, who tell stories with resonance and depth that both children and adults can respond to. Once in a literature course, I lapsed back into Keats' "The Eve of St. Agnes" and realized how much more effective "Snowbound," with its sense of nature and place in America, of loss and reclamation, would have been. The students, with relief, went on to read Whitman.

The directness in American writing and its use of the native idiom have helped to create the spirit of modern English. The modern spirit in the West, besides taking its situations from ordinary life, used the language of ordinary life alongside a more formal vocabulary. With greater consistency than European literature, American prose and poetry mixed the domestic, the humble, with the cerebral. Emily Dickinson's poetry waited in obscurity until the world could catch up with such mixtures as "The soul selects her own society, / Then shuts the door." Again Emerson was a prophet: "I embrace the common. I explore and sit at the feet of the familiar." American literature not only took up a vernacular but celebrated it. And its creation of a modern spirit found a brilliant twentieth-century expression in the Anglo-American poet W. H. Auden. After a philosophical *tour de force* in the poem "Many Happy Returns," the poet admonishes the birthday child to "Live beyond your income, / Travel for enjoyment, / Follow your own nose." The aesthetics of modernism, lost in some contemporary writing, have meant "natural words in their natural order." In that America pioneered.

In revitalizing our language, by reading and writing it, we secure a freedom in a world more and more encumbered by restraints. Freedom of speech may die from its own disuse. As language atrophies, the myth of individuality seeks more and more the exercise of power, of one man over another, while the civilized do a slow dance of resignation. The craze for picture taking, tape recording, tennis playing, travel, camping, and all the other bursts of energy on the American scene will not be enough to allow enough of us to feel free. The myth of our nation—that *all men are created equal* and are worth the promise of God—puts a terrible burden on us to be someone. "I'm nobody. Who are you? / Are you nobody too? / Then there's a pair of us. / Don't tell—they'd banish us, you know," Emily Dickinson wrote in defiance of what has now become celebrity. "How dreary to be somebody. / How public—like a frog— / To tell your name the livelong June / To an admiring bog." Add to the emphasis on the individual his loneliness in a disorganized society, his uprootedness from the culture of his sires, and the need for American reading and writing is self-evident. Writing, even of memos, diaries, or correspondence, gives the individual a sense of control, however intangible or real, over his destiny. Without writing, many Americans feel hobbled or hollow without knowing why.

In American literature of two centuries, Americans cannot merely hear their history, not merely gain or enlarge a sense of place, not merely touch the much vaunted identity Americans crave, but become more comfortable with themselves. American literature offers a language suitable to our needs today. Americans from Dickinson to Hemingway, writing in a style as spare as a spindle chair, were the founders of the modern movement. While writers in other cultures have experimented with natural speech, with domestic idiom, our literature has possessed a native idiom for over a century. How important is the infusion of plain American talk in Thoreau and Dickinson. How fluent is the dialect that schoolmarms chide in Twain and Faulkner. As teachers who teach American literature know, it is a literature that students, given the chance, read avidly. One hundred and twenty-five years after the publication of *Walden,* we can now claim American literature for what it is—a definition of the inner life of our country, of its experience and character. For against a culture of optimism—coming from the television studio and the advertisement in the feeble form of slickness, telling us that the jackpot can and will be hit—American writing tells us that the dream is both more substantial and essentially difficult. By knowing Emily Dickinson, for instance, Americans could know that ritual is finally internal. "After great pain, a formal feeling comes." Literature reveals nuance; ill-read, Americans miss the subtle. In Wallace Stevens, they could find the search for form: "Clear water in a brilliant bowl, / Pink and white carnations. The light / In the room more like a snowy air, / Reflecting snow. A newly-fallen snow / At the end of winters when afternoons return. / Pink and white carnations—one desires / So much more than that." Why, when poetry is still taught, do we begin with "The Ancient Mariner" when we have Edward Arlington Robinson's "Mr. Flood's Party," when in Robinson we have an American perfection of metrics?

The virgin continent, Fitzgerald wrote in *The Great Gatsby*, "had once pandered in whispers to the last and greatest of all human dreams; for a transitory enchanted moment man must have held his breath in the presence of this continent, compelled into an aesthetic contemplation he neither understood nor desired, face to face for the last time in history with something commensurate to his capacity for wonder." To a country at last waking up to its difficulties, American literature should come as a cooling in the night, a relief in the recognition of a shared reality. American literature lets us be honest with ourselves; it allows us to accept the bad news of American life in whatever sunlight we can find. And in allowing us to be honest, it can allow us to write.

Some would say that in a country as diverse in population and geography as the United States, there can be no national literature, no American culture. But different as are mountains and plains, rivers and oceans, differing though we are in ethnicity or in race, the American adventure has imposed conditions that have shaped national character. Though only the first settlers were Puritans, those who followed necessarily became that too. How else in a new, strange, and sometimes hostile land could a man or woman prove his worth except by self-endeavor or righteousness? We are all Puritans and we are all plutocrats. For as we have striven upward, from farm and slum, from grade school and correspondence courses, we have known the corruption of Calvinists on the altar of power or money—our worth determined by a sign of the world. Neither geography nor ethnicity stands in the way of our problems and our character, as American novels testify. Hawthorne's early New Englanders, not only severe but sometimes radiant, find their heirs in Willa Cather's Nebraska pioneers, Slavic and Bohemian, large as well as small in spirit. The faith of Ernest in Hawthorne's "The Great Stone Face" shines in the trust of a grandfather, the generosity of women in Cather's stories. From Hawthorne's "The Great Carbuncle" to Fitzgerald's *The Great Gatsby,* an inner life of romantic striving proceeds, even to corruption and death. Telling us of our difficulties, American literature holds us to our better values; and in both lets us know we are in good company.

Hear, for an American style and an American outlook, perorations in two profoundly American novels, one about a modern man in urban America, the other about a pioneer woman in Ohio of the early nineteenth century. Saul Bellow's Herzog, in the novel of that name (1964), speaks, after many dislocations, about his life.

> Anyway, can I pretend I have much choice? I look at myself and see chest, thighs, feet—a head. This strange organization, I know it will die. And inside—something, something, happiness. . . . "Thou movest me." That leaves no choice. Something produces intensity, a holy feeling, as oranges produce orange, as grass green, as birds heat. Some hearts put out more love and some less of it, presumably. Does it signify anything? There are those who say this product of hearts is knowledge. "Je sens mon coeur et je connais les hommes." But this mind now detached itself also from its French. I

couldn't say that, for sure. My face too blind, my mind too limited, my instincts too narrow. But this intensity, doesn't it mean anything? Is it an idiot joy that makes this animal, the most peculiar animal of all, exclaim something? And he thinks this reaction a sign, a proof, of eternity? And he has it in his breast? "Thou movest me." "But what do you want, Herzog?" But that's just it—not a solitary thing. I am pretty well satisfied to be, to be just as it is willed, and for as long as I may remain in occupancy.

In *The Trees* (1940), the first book in the remarkable trilogy about the settlement of Ohio followed by *The Fields* and *The Town* and called together *The Awakening Land,* Conrad Richter wrote in the voice of a young woman who had braved, by foot, migration from Pennsylvania, settlement by clearing a wilderness, loss of a younger sister to Indians. The idiom and the outlook are, like Bellow's, American. Out of the land and culture in which these two quite different writers have lived, an Emersonian briskness— an idiom honoring the domestic, the humble, the natural— and an Emersonian fire—burning through—emerges. Hear Sayward Luckett, the pioneer girl:

Let the good come, Sayward thought, for the bad would come of its own self. Never again would they see the face of their little Sullie, for if she wasn't dead, some Indians far off in the vasty Northwest country had her. But a young one of her own was on the way, and if it came a girl, they could call her Sullie and look on her face. That's how life was, death and birth, grub and harvest, rain and clearing, winter and summer. You had to take one with the other, for that's the way it ran.

Surpassing ethnicity, time, and place, American literature speaks of American situations. White readers as well as black sit in stunned attention to a reading of Ellison's *The Invisible Man,* Freudian and biblical, a successor to *Moby Dick* and *Native Son.* Bellow and Malamud, among Jewish American writers perhaps the most lasting, speak to a wide audience because they create individuals in the grip of a common time.

Bellow, thinking of himself as an American writer, shuns the easy literary label of "Jewish American" novelist, confesses a debt to his own experience, his city of Chicago, his own life of the mind. *The Assistant* by Malamud speaks for the little man in mid-century overcome by bigness, kept human by helping to redeem the more miserable. Chaim Potok's *The Chosen* circulates from lending libraries in New England villages. While literature has always reached into the particular to illuminate the general, in America it reaches into particular ethnicities and places to create a national consciousness. From Ahab and Ishmael in *Moby Dick*, the darkness and light in American literature still spins. Both embody prototypes of American character, the first by obsession, the second by trust and the humor to explore. Ahab also resides in a doctor's manse in Henry James's *Washington Square*, while Ishmael is generous with newcomers on Willa Cather's Great Divide.

Not only ethnic but regional creations reach a national definition. While from Massachusetts came the first stream of American literature, the South has brought forth much of twentieth-century genius. Until recently at least, our writers have kept a network of cultures alive. In 1903 Henry James wrote, "How can everything so have gone that the only 'Southern' book of any distinction published for many a year is *The Souls of Black Folk*, by that most accomplished of members of the Negro race, Mr. W. E. B. Du Bois."

In American literature—in *Souls of Black Folk*, as in the writing of Richard Wright and Ralph Ellison—social questions find human dimension and attain the stature of poetry. In *U.S.A.*, Dos Passos made a novel out of an impassioned political viewpoint. Outside of Jack London, where we find clear-cut adventure, social protest does not wind up in caricature. Steinbeck teaches a deep political science, because his forces of society play with plausible human possibilities. Out of the tortured South, not only Faulkner but also Carson McCullers makes a stark interplay of character, warped and regular. In the stirring *Ceremonies of Dark Old Men* by the black playwright Lonne Elder III, the great themes used by

Eugene O'Neill express joy and tragedy in Harlem. O'Neill, the one indisputably great American playwright, walks us on a tightrope between reality and illusion, warning us of the perils of both. The complexity, rather than a caricature of businessmen, comes forth in Howells, the pathos of commercial hope not only in Arthur Miller but also in Sinclair Lewis. A Puritan conscience in *Silas Lapham* helps the mighty to resign and to rise again. Lewis's *Babbitt* is lured to Thoreau's wilderness and fulfilled, briefly, there. In both the American and international novels of Henry James, we find an American bedrock—a dogged responsibility that forces the innocent, even when they become aware, to carry a burden they chose. There is no more astute psychological study of American feminism or more of a "great American novel" than James's *The Bostonians* (1886).

So far, American education, while complaining of the results, has left the discovery of the American self to popular culture. In their costumes of Indians and overalls, in their hairdos of African and Indian chiefs, in soul music and at rock concerts, young Americans stumble toward their past without the guidance of an educated hand. The new interest in and affinity for the American Indian are reasonable—yet pathetic. Not only the Indian, but the direct ancestors and the wounded selves of many Americans as well are ignored in schoolbooks. The Indian becomes a harmless symbol of the dispossession many have felt. Yet dispossession and courage in the face of it are abundant in American letters. Frost, thought by some so rural in his imagery that he is lost to urban students, speaks not only in a clean American language but also about situations urban students know well. Frost's characters face poverty, and grope in the dark of misunderstanding. A Puerto Rican boy in my class found Silas, the homeless hired man in "The Death of the Hired Man," a lost relative of his; while a black girl distinguished herself with a brilliant analysis of the tension between husband and wife in "Home Burial." An Orthodox Jewish student found in Conrad Richter's *The Trees* an intriguing manifestation of the matriarchal strength he saw around him. O'Neill's *Long Day's Journey into Night* opened more worlds than had hallucinatory drugs to one class; and a girl reported that her unschooled mother, to whom she had brought it in eagerness, found the play "utterly true." There is response to American writers. In an evening class of older students, *Poor Richard's Almanack* and the pieties and witticisms therein, spoke directly to their sense of striving and brought forth their sense of humor. Marvelous parodies were written of Poor Richard's sayings. Of Whitman, a black girl in another class wrote: "He was composed of beauty and ugliness. He had love and hatred in him. There was pain and happiness in Whitman. All these elements made Whitman the unique person that he was . . . he could see meaning in a blade of grass, he could get a message from a flower, he could feel the sadness of a star and compare it with his own. He could then put these things into poetry."

Given Hawthorne's tales to read, students perceive common ills—common strengths of humanity magnified, understandable and interesting. Out of a discussion on Hawthorne's "The Birthmark," a girl whose innocence I had overestimated asked if it wasn't like a story by Edgar Allan Poe. Another student objected, among other things, to what he called "old English" and defiantly said he couldn't read Hawthorne. The sensitive young black—a kind of Hawthornian character himself—suggested a reason for such objections. He claimed that a word like "anon" stopped him completely and made it impossible to read on; I told him he took such words as a personal affront, when they weren't; that he could read around those few words, as all of us have done with words we haven't known right off, and understand the passage. Sensitive to everything, including racism, he took the inclusion of words he didn't understand as a form of exclusion. Hawthorne, he thought, seemed to discriminate against him. Two days later he came back, saying what I thought he might say, once he gave Hawthorne's great tale "The Artist of the Beautiful" a chance. "That's a fantastic story. Why, that story is about me." Wrote a girl about Hawthorne, "His selection of words is like the paint

an artist skillfully blends to create different moods."
Using American literature works.

The world opened up for one student who had discovered *Huckleberry Finn.* To Mencken, the bad boy of American journalism in his time, the discovery of Twain's novel, which he reread every year, had been a "stupendous event." This new disciple, the son of Italian immigrants, had found in Twain a critic of parochialism to help him let off steam and nurture an original outlook. The adventures of a nineteenth-century river boy had offered him a constructive outlet for his own tensions. "I studied and absorbed his whole philosophy of life and strove to emulate him," he wrote in a paper. "I built primitive shelters, picked and ate berries, and lazied among the sumac and pines of the Cross Island [the parkway near his home]."

We still do not possess enough respect for our own past, an understanding that it is our present. "Our day of dependence, our long apprenticeship to the learning of other lands," Emerson declared in 1837, "draws to a close." Surely come of age, American literature deserves to be the basic literature offered by American high schools and colleges, as a revelation of the inner life of a nation, as a study of American imagination and conflict. Shakespeare need not be lost, nor Donne and Marvell; they can be worked back to, especially by those who have learned to care. The study of literature need not be the esoteric pursuit of the few that it now is; it can be the common property of us all, a record of our humanity and spirit.

After reading *The Great Gatsby,* a white student in an Open Admissions class wrote a response to "The American Dream":

> The "American Dream" is a dream that has at its roots, meglomania. The American is always striving for more, working hard to preserve this Protestant ethic. He holds tightly to what he has accumulated. When in conversation, he lets his status drift up slowly like a helium baloon let go by a child.

I remember an occasion, a year ago, in which I had visited an old friend. His mother invited me into their living room for some conversation. She told me that her husband had just passed a test and received a job that many men were turned away from. I inquired, "Of what nature is this job?" She replied, "He is working for the Sanitation Department." I cast a bewildered stare at her direction and resumed conversation.

I couldn't help but wonder why she had built her husband up. Why didn't she just explain that her husband was simply a garbage collector. I exchanged thoughts with her son and embarked on my walk home.

As soon as my foot hit the asphalt street, a huge car zipped by and came to a sudden stop. After the tires stopped screeching I looked to recover my leg. But alas it was still there. I recognized the driver of the car. He was a friend of mine, taking his father's car out for a spin. "Hop in," he said. I accompanied him hoping to get a ride home.

Instead of getting a ride home, I received a list of all the accessories the luxury liner contained, and the price of each. I also received a description of the superfluous gadgets the vehicle would contain in the near future. After he gave me a few guided tours of the neighborhood, he let me off. In his closing remark he confided to me that he was getting an "outrageous tape deck" soon.

I entered my room and fell on my bed, exhausted from the day's events. I still can't comprehend why people are out to impress me. It appears to me that most Americans are looking for a round of applause, something to make them feel at ease, a public reaction to secure their shaky hand. Because of this need for sanction, we loudmouth our illusions. We too easily become great actors and forget our true parts. . . .

Gatsby exhibited his possessions because after cutting himself from his roots that's all he owned. The people who I have written about have caught the American virus and will continue to infect their children with it. Why can't Americans come down to size?

In no nation has there been a culture of affirmation, though popular religions in America have tried for such a creation. But the articulate young today find their identity in a shriller voice of protest than did their predecessors. The writer of this paper, unstudied in his attire, trailing long hair, had the face of Portnoy in the hairdo of William Penn. America breeds physical as well as spiritual heirs to its founders. Yet it is a measure of our decline that such romantic revolutionaries as he can barely turn their criticism toward statement of a principle. To bring America "down to size"—that's a wise updating of Thoreau's admonition to simplify. This student's piece, like our larger literature, met the realities of the world, but without the courage of a double vision. "I condemn and affirm, say no and yes, say yes and say no," concludes the hero of Ellison's *The Invisible Man* after his journey through racism, through a surrealism of political and industrial life. Ours is a literature of particular protest because popular principles are always denied by the world. In its criticism, American literature is always raising popular principle to a lofty stand. For the commonplaces still prevalent in American life, we have literary elaborations and analysis. "Money isn't everything." For that platitude read Thoreau's: "A man is rich in proportion to the number of things he can afford to leave alone." Americans still put great stress on character and value it more than "brains." Emerson, the sage, codified the popular sentiment when he wrote, "Character is higher than intellect." Americans really still like heroes in their fiction. Henry James declared that the challenge to a novelist viewing his characters was to see "deep difficulty braved"; and out of braving such difficulties, his heroines and heroes live. Contrary to the popularly held notion, literature is not highfalutin. It is only when a people of one culture are asked to flock to the culture of another, as Americans are to English.

9 Illiteracy or Literacy

In a society where the telephone replaces the personal letter, and television the reading of newspapers and books, people begin to assume that writing isn't necessary. As a teacher I am ashamed of having to remind students that many jobs require some kind of writing—memos, letters, reports. Most of what is heard on television—news, comedy shows, soap opera—and what is seen at the movies—is written first. But the "difficulty" of writing is becoming fixed in the minds of the young. One student of mine argued for the superiority of the tape recorder over writing; a tape from a soldier to his mother, he held, was the highest form of communication.

Without writing, we are less alive. Writing is the indispensable extension of the self, the mind and the personality. We are less civilized without writing, because our thoughts are not subject to development, to organization. The more persuasively a person writes, the more persuasively he will speak. But we will always be capable of better expressing our ideas in writing than in speech. A friend of mine used to say he could not "think without a typewriter." I know what he means. Writing is so much a trainer of the mind that thought can hardly be said to exist without it.

Yet everywhere language is in disarray. Enter an American living room and discover the absence of domestic culture —no one talks, the television blares. The invention required of conversation is lost to the mind-replacing TV.

The Bible, once a model of the use and the power of language, has undergone changes, succumbing to the impoverishment of modern versions and scholarly accuracy. For the great lines of the King James version of Ecclesiastes, "that the race is not to the swift, nor the battle to the strong, neither yet bread to the wise, nor yet riches to men of understanding, nor yet favor to men of skill; but time and chance happeneth to all," the widely used New English Bible reduces resonance and meaning: "Speed does not win the race, nor strength the battle. Bread does not belong to the wise, nor wealth to the intelligent, nor success to the skillful; time and chance govern all." Biblical revisions, such as this one, have been mangled by the hands of pharisees, who underrate what people can understand, who deprive them of the beauty of poetic language. It is all a sign of the bad times.

Reading less, knowing less, we are fast on the way to becoming an illiterate nation, unable to write, unable to think, but able to take tests. The time may come when, like countries we used to call "backward," we will have such a high rate of illiteracy that we can apply that term to ourselves. We cannot go on certifying Americans as literate when they can only read or write at a basic level.

We cannot abolish television, but we can restore written college entrance exams. If students had to write substantial essays on entrance exams, then writing would reestablish itself in high school curriculum. The Educational Testing Service and the other testing companies maintain that objective tests, graded by machine, are the only practical method of testing college aptitude. If it really proved uneconomic for the private testing services to pay readers of written exams, then the federal government should come to the aid of writing. Surely writing is in the national interest, and the decline in writing ability a national disaster. Federal funds could not be spent for a more important national purpose than subsidizing the reading of written exams.

If the tyranny of objective testing were removed, who would teach writing in our schools? Instead of installing more electronic equipment, the wise agencies of our land—from local to state and federal government—could use funds for small writing classes, not more than twenty students in each. Journalists and professional writers could be encouraged to teach along with dedicated teachers already within the system. What is needed in teaching is connection—between the life of language and the life of a people.

In the early years of Open Admissions, a white student, unschooled in writing and wary of it, wrote a memorable parable. At the beginning of the course, he misspelled with pride and wrote confused sentences. Neither shaving regularly nor growing a beard, wearing a lumberjacket and boots, he walked out of one frontier and into another—a guest at Andrew Jackson's inaugural becoming his own stylist, his own ecologist. His piece was entitled "Old Turtle Road."

I was driving down the Long Island Expressway, when my 1955 Dodge exhausted itself. So now it was up to me to get to my destination, Jericho. I was walking for what seemed to be hundreds of miles, until I rested. Lying by a road sign on the side of the road, I saw a turtle. Not that seeing a turtle is strange, just rare.

The turtle came towards me, until he was standing by my arm. I glanced down, and to my amazement, the turtle said hello. Now, this doesn't happen everyday, and I knew this turtle was rare and weird. At first I didn't know what to do, say hello or say goodbye. So I just ignored him. But again he said hello and this time I answered. "What did you say?" The turtle answered with another hello. Well obviously, I thought, he doesn't have a large vocabulary.

But as he started talking, I knew I was wrong. He told me of his home, which had been covered with tar. And that now he was a resident of the Long Island Expressway. His family was now imprisoned under the asphalt ceiling. He had been fishing while all this happened, some seven years ago. And he really didn't know where his home was, for so many things have changed.

So I gave him a ride on the back of my pack. And all the while he told me of years before. When the only danger was dodging the cows in the field. He told me of those fields, of green grass that to him was as tall as the sky. The sky was clean and clear.

As the day was drawing to a close, I reached my aunt's home. I asked her if he could live out his life in her yard. As I left, I thought of my friend, that his life now won't be so terribly hard. I thought of his family, and the families of others, that the Long Island Expressway had evicted or imprisoned. I thought of creatures even smaller than turtles, and creatures larger than me, that the world has covered with tar.

If we honored writing, we would honor ourselves.

110074